Author photo © Desiree Adams

Lee Newbery lives with his son and dog in a seaside town in West Wales. By day he works for an arts charity, helping people to share their stories through creative writing, painting and participatory arts, and by night he sits down at his laptop to write.

Lee enjoys adventuring, drinking ridiculous amounts of tea, and giving his dog a good cuddle – or a *cwtch*, as they say in Wales. His first book, *The Last Firefox*, was shortlisted for the Waterstones Children's Book Prize.

BOOKS BY LEE NEWBERY

The Last Firefox

The First Shadowdragon

The Lost Sunlion

Praise for THE LAST FIREFOX series:

'Magical' *Sunday Express*

'Comic, adventurous and charming' *Guardian*

'Funny, sweet and charming – a real delight!'
SAM COPELAND, author of
Charlie Changes Into a Chicken

'Utterly gorgeous storytelling . . . *The Last
Firefox* will long burn bright in your heart'
JENNY PEARSON, author of
The Super Miraculous Journey of Freddie Yates

'Crackles with adventure and love'
MARIA KUZNIAR, author of *The Ship of Shadows*

'An enchanting fantasy adventure as warm
as a firefox's tail . . . a joyous gem!'
LESLEY PARR, author of *The Valley of Lost Secrets*

'A heart (and tail!) warming adventure about family,
friendship and one flamin' cute fox cub'
___ ___ ___ ___ ___ 'er

LEE NEWBERY

THE LOST SUN LION

ILLUSTRATED BY **LAURA CATALÁN**

PUFFIN

PUFFIN BOOKS

UK | USA | Canada | Ireland | Australia
India | New Zealand | South Africa

Puffin Books is part of the Penguin Random House group of companies
whose addresses can be found at global.penguinrandomhouse.com

www.penguin.co.uk
www.puffin.co.uk
www.ladybird.co.uk

First published 2024

001

Set in 13/20pt Bembo Book MT Std
Typeset by Jouve (UK), Milton Keynes
Printed and bound in Great Britain by Clays Ltd, Elcograf S.p.A.

The authorized representative in the EEA is Penguin Random House Ireland,
Morrison Chambers, 32 Nassau Street, Dublin D02 YH68

A CIP catalogue record for this book is available from the British Library

ISBN: 978–0–241–62858–4

All correspondence to:
Puffin Books
Penguin Random House Children's
One Embassy Gardens, 8 Viaduct Gardens, London SW11 7BW

For my lovely Nan and Gramps,
under whose roof I penned my first little stories.

Chapter 1

When you first get a firefox, nobody warns you about the firefox zoomies. They're like ordinary zoomies except, well . . . fiery. And after three weeks of being stuck in the house, the firefox zoomies start to get a bit, let's just say, *explosive*.

'Noooooo! Not my prize-winning tea cosy!'

A comet whizzes past me, bounces off the back of the sofa like a pinball, then catapults across the room. I ignore it and keep slotting my trading cards into their little sleeves, like I've been doing for the last two hours, while the rain continues to hammer away at the windows.

I have come to realize that the best way to deal with the firefox zoomies is to pretend they aren't happening.

My pa has not learned this lesson.

He skids into the room, his expression one of utter desperation. I can tell he's trying to catch Cadno and rescue the scrap of wool between his jaws, but the cub is moving too fast. He makes two laps of the coffee table in the time it takes to blink, then shoots through Pa's legs and into the hall in a trail of flames.

'Charlie, do something!' Pa gasps.

I slowly close my trading-card file, place my hands on my lap and look up. 'Oh, hello, Pa. How nice to see you.'

'You have to get my tea cosy back!' Pa cries, dashing my attempt at pleasantries. 'It took me a week to knit. Doesn't that mean anything to you?'

Frankly, it doesn't. I don't understand why a teapot needs to wear a coat when it gets filled with boiling water and probably just wants to cool down. But this is clearly very important to Pa, so I give him a sympathetic look.

'Erm, of course it does,' I say. 'But, Pa . . . it is too late for your tea cosy. The only thing you can do is accept it and move on.'

As though backing up my statement, a sudden puff of light illuminates the hallway behind Pa, like a mini explosion has just taken place, followed by a delighted yip.

Pa hangs his head. The tea cosy is no more.

'I'm sorry for your loss,' I tell him. 'Maybe you can knit another one that's even better?'

Pa nods, but he doesn't look like he means it. I pat the space on the sofa next to me.

'Do you want to help me sort out my trading cards?'

Pa shakes his head.

'Where's Dad?'

'He's upstairs, trying to make a giant hamster wheel,' says Pa with a sigh. 'Something for Cadno to spend his energy on until we can go outside.'

We lapse into silence. Pa's gaze moves to the living-room window, a blur of spitting, watery grey.

'When is it ever going to end?' he finally says. 'It's been ages now. Surely this isn't normal?'

'You remember we live in Wales, right?'

'I know that, but even we don't usually get *this* much rain. It hasn't stopped, has it? Not even for a second.'

He's right. It started in the middle of what had been a sunny day. There wasn't any rain forecast, but the clouds just rolled across the sky into a moody grey ceiling that blocked out the sun, and then the droplets started falling.

And haven't stopped since.

That was last month, and things are starting to get out of hand. The river has burst its banks, slowly swallowing the surrounding fields, and the castle on the hill has practically become an island. School closed a week ago after the grounds flooded, and part of the canteen roof collapsed under the weight of all the water.

We've been stuck at home ever since, watching the minutes creep by. I haven't been able to see my best mates, Lippy and Roo, nor have I been able to take Cadno out. The last time we got caught in a rainstorm, his fire dimmed and we had to run home. He was weak for hours afterwards. Firefoxes and water do *not* mix.

Weather experts are calling it a freak phenomenon, and it's showing no signs of stopping. Neither are Cadno's zoomies. If anything, both the rain and the zoomies only seem to be getting more and more intense. The zoomies started not long after the rain did, and we've had many household casualties since. Pa's tea cosy, countless socks, a throw, a lampshade, enough teddy bears for a whole picnic, and even a couple of cushions.

'I haven't once been able to take Edie out to try her new raincoat,' Pa laments.

He reaches behind him and grabs a pink coat, covered in rainbows and glossy from lack of use. It's still got the price tag on.

Cadno slinks back into the room and, refusing to

5

meet Pa's eye, hops on to the sofa and curls into a ball on my lap. I place my hand on his belly, still hot from the excitement of destroying Pa's tea cosy, and gradually feel his flames cool beneath my fingertips until he starts to snore, his energy spent for another half-hour or so.

Pa sits himself down on the sofa, muttering about how we're all starting to lose our minds, when the TV lights up. I had anime on in the background as I was sorting through my cards, but it's automatically switched to what looks like a news bulletin.

The words *EMERGENCY ANNOUNCE-MENT* flash across the screen in red.

'What's going on?' I ask.

Pa looks troubled. He shoots me what I think is supposed to be a comforting smile but just ends up looking like he's got gas. He hurries to the bottom of the stairs.

'Honey?' he calls up. 'I think you might want to come down.'

'Now?' Dad's voice drifts from the spare bedroom.

'But I've almost finished! You're not going to believe what I've made. Cadno will never want to go for a walk ever again —'

'Let me rephrase,' Pa replies. '*Get your butt down here right now, or I'll —*'

But Dad has already appeared at the top of the stairs, a flailing Edie in his arms. 'All right, all right, I'm here,' he says, quickly descending with a worried look on his face. 'What's the matter, dear? You just used your Angry Pa voice.'

'Just go into the living room and sit down,' Pa growls through gritted teeth. 'There's something weird on TV.'

Dad obeys and comes over to sit next to me. He gives me a *what's up with him?* sort of look. All I manage is a shrug before a news reporter appears on the screen, her expression sombre.

Behind her is a live video of a lake, the waters dark and choppy as the rain drives down. It switches to a bloated river that's being fed by a powerful jet of water which erupts from an enormous pipe, and then, lastly, to a scene showing a towering stone wall that runs from one side of a valley to the other, with water gushing over the edge and into the river far below.

'Wait a minute,' says Dad. 'Isn't that –'

'We are coming live to you this morning from the Llyn Reservoir,' the news reporter begins, 'just five miles north of the rural farming town of Bryncastell, where unprecedented rainfall is the cause of growing concern.'

The video cuts to a close-up of the dam wall, where a crack has appeared in the stone near the rim. We often take Cadno for walks at the Llyn Reservoir – or used to before this rain started. We've stood on the walkway atop the dam countless times, clutching the railings, peering over at the dizzying drop below.

The walkway is gone now. Water surges over it, cascading down the dam in a mighty waterfall.

'I'm here with the local mayor, Gavin Howells,' the reporter goes on, and the shot zooms out to show a man with worry lines all over his face sitting next to her. 'Mr Howells, what is the problem?'

The mayor shuffles uncomfortably. 'W-well, we haven't seen rainfall like this since records began,' he stammers, 'and, as such, the dam – which was built almost a century ago, I might add – has never experienced such pressure from the reservoir. If the rain doesn't stop soon, we're worried that it might . . .'

He peters out into a strained silence.

'Burst?' the reporter puts in.

The mayor winces. 'No. Well, y-yes. But we absolutely do not want anybody to panic –'

'And what would a breach in the dam mean for the villages and towns that lie in the valley below the reservoir, Mr Howells?'

'Oh, it would be catastrophic,' the mayor replies, then gasps, like he's said the wrong thing. 'But that's a worst-case scenario!'

The news reporter's eyes glint hungrily. I can tell that she's mining for the juiciest possible story, even if it means stirring fear – which I can already feel beginning to churn in the pit of my belly.

'Mr Howells, this part of Wales has a history of

villages being flooded so that valleys could be turned into reservoirs,' she goes on. 'Are you saying history might be about to repeat itself? Could Bryncastell be about to meet the same fate as some of its counterparts?'

'There is a very small possibility, and I mean *tiny*, so tiny it's barely a possibility at all,' the mayor replies, holding up a pinched forefinger and thumb, 'that Bryncastell could get flooded when the dam – I mean, *if* the dam bursts. But we are monitoring the situation closely and we have emergency measures in place to evacuate in plenty of time, should such an occasion arise, which it *won't* –'

'But it *is* a possibility?'

Mr Howells's shoulders drop in defeat. 'Yes,' he says, with a sigh.

'Thank you for your time, Mr Howells,' says the reporter. She returns her attention to the camera. 'Stay tuned for hourly updates on the crisis at the Llyn Reservoir. But now it's time for the weather with Lisa . . .'

The image switches to a big map of Bryncastell and the surrounding county and a red-haired woman standing before it.

'Thank you, Karen. Well, I'm sorry to say that there doesn't seem to be an end in sight when it comes to this rain –'

The screen turns black. My heart pounds into the silence. Even Edie seems to have sensed the change in atmosphere – she just sits on Dad's lap, quietly sucking her thumb.

'It's just scaremongering,' says Dad, putting the

remote back down on the coffee table. 'The dam isn't going to burst. It's made from metres-thick stone, for goodness' sake. Not even a giant could make a dent in it.'

'But, Dad –'

Dad holds his hand up. 'Pay it no more mind, Charlie. You heard the mayor. There's no need to panic. They're monitoring the situation.'

'I don't know,' says Pa, who looks a bit queasy. 'Maybe we should pack some bags, just in case . . .'

Dad snorts. 'Will you listen to yourself? This is what they *want*. To make sure we all freak out so we stay glued to our tellies. Well, not in this household! Anyway, come on. I've got something to show you!'

Dad gets to his feet and heads back upstairs with Edie still in his arms. Pa and I exchange nervous glances. Cadno leaps off my lap and across the room, his fire already dancing over his fur, regenerated even by just a few minutes' sleep.

Pa and I dutifully follow.

'In here!' comes Dad's voice from the spare room.

We enter and find him standing proudly before what I can only describe as the most peculiar object I've ever seen. 'I present to you ... the Firefox Rambler Three-Sixty!'

The Firefox Rambler 360 appears to be an old washing basket. It's propped on a spindle made from various rod-like utensils from around the house: a mop, a broom and the crutches from the time Dad broke his leg trying to do a backflip on our old trampoline.

It looks *vaguely* like a giant hamster wheel. Or something that's trying really hard to be a giant hamster wheel but didn't quite understand the assignment.

'Well, what do you think?' Dad asks, his expression puppyish with hope.

The thing with Dad is that he gets excited about new projects all the time, but they never turn out quite the way they're supposed to.

'It . . . er . . . it definitely has that rustic, home-made charm you're so good at, sweetie,' says Pa. 'So what does it . . . I mean, can it . . . ?'

'Ah, you're lost for words,' says Dad, beaming proudly. 'Understandable. Look, I'll show you. Cadno, hop on!'

He beckons Cadno. The cub takes a cautious step forward, gives the contraption a testing sniff, then climbs on to the wheel. He baulks when the frame wobbles slightly, but Dad makes a comforting cooing sound.

'Don't worry, it's perfectly safe. Now, you just start running . . .'

Cadno reluctantly breaks into a trot, with his tail between his legs and his head hanging low, almost like he's embarrassed. I have to stifle a laugh — he looks ridiculous. He's grown over the last few months, so the wheel is just a bit too small for him, the whole thing squeaking and shuddering like it's about to fall apart at any second.

Dad claps his hands in triumph. 'That's it! You're doing it, Cadno! Keep going, boy!'

Cadno keeps running, his confidence growing. His tail lifts, his tongue lolling excitedly from his mouth, as his legs start to blur beneath him.

Edie lets out an overjoyed shriek. 'Go, Cadno! Go, Cadno!'

'I knew I was on to something with this one!' Dad grins, wrapping his arms round Pa's shoulders like he's just invented something that could make us millions. 'Brilliant, isn't it? We never need to worry about bad weather ever again!'

Cadno barks in agreement, and even I have to admit that Dad seems to have done a good job. Cadno looks like he's having more fun than he's had since the rain began.

Then his fur sparks.

And I don't mean with his usual fiery sparks, I mean proper *electric* sparks.

I blink. 'Hey, did anybody else see –'

It happens again. This time a tiny bolt of lightning ripples across his fur with a *bang* that makes Edie squeal. *Actual* lightning, like the sort you get forking from the sky during a storm. In fact, when I look closer, his whole body seems to be shimmering with mini rods of flickering electricity, his former flames nowhere in sight.

Pa, Dad and I gawp at each other, completely speechless.

'He's generating electricity,' Dad mutters in disbelief. Then his face gets more animated. 'This is unbelievable! I knew I was good at inventing things, but I didn't realize I was *that* good.'

He grabs Pa's hand and starts dancing him round in a circle. Pa doesn't look very happy about it.

'Erm, I don't think that's –'

'This is ground breaking!' Dad laughs. 'I've invented a way to generate electricity by exercising your pets! Oh my gosh, we're going to be rolling in cash!'

'Dad!' I cry.

Dad comes to a standstill, letting go of a very dizzy-looking Pa.

'What?' he asks.

'I don't think it's your invention that's doing this,' I say.

'What do you mean?'

'I mean, *look*.'

I gesture back at the wheel, which is now slowing

as Cadno eases his pace. He hops off, but the electricity doesn't stop. It keeps sparking round his body even as he sits down on the carpet.

'What's up with him?' asks Pa, his voice squeaky with alarm. 'What's happened to his fire?'

'I don't know,' I reply, and then I address Cadno directly. 'Cadno, where's your fire gone, boy? Show us your fire.'

Cadno tilts his head, then closes his eyes in concentration. We all take a step back, readying ourselves for the blaze of heat, but instead the room fills with an ominous, building crackle. Cadno's whole body is now enveloped in lightning bolts which look like they're about to –

'Take cover!' Pa screams.

We all leap through the door and cower on the landing as Cadno explodes into a dome of electric energy. Lightning crackles across the walls, blackens the curtains, swallows the Firefox Rambler 360. It's like somebody has unleashed a thunderstorm in our spare room.

And then, just like that, it's gone. Silence settles back over the house, and the blinding light fades to nothingness.

We peer inside and find Cadno sitting in the middle of a smoky room, looking very confused. His flames are still nowhere to be seen.

'Looks like we don't have a firefox any more,' I whisper in astonishment. 'We've got an *electrafox*.'

Dad wails. 'My Firefox Rambler Three-Sixty! It's ruined!'

I squint and, through the clearing haze, the wreckage of Dad's invention emerges. It's now just a puddle of molten plastic, the washing basket and crutches merged into a smouldering, unrecognizable mess.

'I'm sorry, honey,' says Pa, giving him a half-hearted pat on the shoulder. 'Meanwhile, I have a very small question ... *WHAT THE FLAMING FIREFOX FARTS JUST HAPPENED TO CADNO?!*'

It's as though he plucked the words right out of my

mouth. Cadno looks like he thinks he might be in trouble.

'Oh, Cadno, don't worry, we're not shouting at you,' I say softly, but when my four-legged friend runs forward for a reassuring cuddle, I hold up my hands. Cadno freezes, eyes wide. 'Wait a minute . . . before you come any closer, are you safe?'

Cadno grunts miserably and sits back down, like he's not quite sure himself. He looks completely lost without his fire.

I glance up at my dads, both of whom look just as confused as I feel. Dad has put Edie on the floor and is pacing back and forth, while Pa is scratching his head and frowning like he's stuck on a tricky crossword clue.

'I don't understand,' he mutters. 'How can he go from being a *fire*fox to an *electra*fox just like that?'

'Something weird is going on,' I say. 'First there's this never-ending rain, then Cadno turning electric . . .'

Pa looks up. 'Wait, you think they're connected?'

I shrug. 'I don't know. But it's two very peculiar

things happening at the same time, isn't it?'

A giggle draws our attention to the floor. We look down in unison, to where Edie is reaching out to touch Cadno's fur. Pa gasps in horror.

'EDIE, NO!'

We're too late – her fingers latch on to Cadno's fur. I clamp my eyes shut, my heart catching in my throat, and wait for a bang, but it doesn't come. Instead, there's more giggling. I open my eyes, and there's Edie, completely un-sizzled, stroking Cadno like she always does, except for one little difference.

I burst out laughing.

'Edie, your hair!'

Edie's hair is standing on end, every single strand poking out or upward, straight as a ruler, like she's rubbed her head against the world's biggest balloon. She chuckles and reaches up to pat her brand-new gravity-defying hairdo.

'It's static from Cadno!' I exclaim.

'Oh, Edie, don't do that to me,' says Pa, clutching his heart.

I join Edie at Cadno's side. I reach out, tentatively at first, and feel that familiar tingle leap into my fingertips. The hairs on my forearm stand on end. And then my hand comes to settle on Cadno's fur, and I don't get zapped. It's different to before. Now, instead of warmth, I feel a soft, electric tickle *pitter-patter* up my arm.

'It's the same as it was with his fire,' I say. 'It can be dangerous when he's angry or excited or scared. But when he's calmer, it's perfectly safe. Here, touch him.'

'Ooh, me, me!' Dad chirrups, bounding forward. 'I want a turn!'

I step aside and Dad leans down, running a hand across Cadno's fur. We all laugh as his hair sticks up. All the fuss seems to cheer the cub up, and even Pa can't help but crack a little smile.

'I still don't understand why this has happened, though,' I say. 'Something doesn't feel right.'

'I agree,' says Pa. 'It doesn't make sense that Cadno would just switch powers like that. I think you're on to something, Charlie. Maybe that and the rain *are* connected.'

I nod. 'I need to make a call. I know a few people who are going to be *very* interested to hear about this.'

Chapter 3

'So he just . . . switched? Just like that?'

The faces of my best mates, Lippy and Roo, collectively known as the Adventure Squad, gawp out at me from my laptop screen. Lippy is in her living room, while Roo is somewhere dark.

'Yep. Dad thought he was generating electricity by running, but it turns out it was coming from *him*.'

Cadno has already given them a display of his new electric powers. I put him down on my bed, propped the laptop on my pillow and went to the other side of the room while Cadno unleashed a trident of lightning bolts that blasted up to the ceiling and left scorch marks on the plaster.

Pa's going to be so annoyed when he notices.

'But . . . but how can he just change like that?' asks Lippy.

'I don't know,' I say. 'But I think I know somebody who will.'

Roo's face lights up. 'Teg?'

I nod.

'You want to go and talk to Teg?' says Lippy. 'But, Charlie, the rain . . . it's dangerous out there. Did you see the news? Bryncastell might end up like all those drowned Welsh villages we learned about in history class!'

She's right. We've had a few lessons on Wales's lost communities – once thriving villages that had to be evacuated in the last century so that the valleys they clustered in could be flooded to make reservoirs for drinking water. And even further back in time, there's another story about a whole bunch of towns that got swallowed up by the sea. The legend calls it Cantre'r Gwaelod.

'I know, it's bad,' I say grimly. 'But I think the rain and Cadno's transformation might be connected. I've seen enough magic to know that when a series of strange things happens around here, they're usually related. And they're usually connected to Fargone.'

Fargone – or the Other Wales, as we sometimes call it – is the magical land where Cadno originally came from, and where lots of our friends live. Like Teg, who started the Gallivant Menagerie, a travelling magical-creature sanctuary. And Branwen, who's now the queen of the whole realm.

'So what are we waiting for?' says Roo. 'Let's go already!'

Lippy and I blink.

Roo scowls. 'What?'

'Well, Roo, no offence, but . . .' I start.

'Come on, out with it!'

'It's just that you don't usually take the lead when

it comes to adventures, do you?' Lippy blurts. 'You usually follow us. You know, a bit like sheep do.'

Roo looks like he's been slapped in the face with a fish. 'A *sheep*? You think I'm a sheep?'

'I think what Lippy means,' I say hastily, 'is that you're usually more sensible than we are, right?'

Lippy nods quickly. 'Yes, that's it, *sensible*!'

Roo slumps. 'You're right. I *am* a sheep. You guys have done all these heroic things. You're Charlie the Legendary, defeater of the Grendilock and Draig. And you're Lippy the Radiant, with this amazing magical bond with Blodyn. I'm just Roo. Roo the Reluctant.'

Lippy and I exchange awkward glances. It's true that the last few times we've been to Fargone, Lippy has formed an even deeper connection with Blodyn the floradoe. They've helped the queendom to flourish again after Draig the shadowdragon leeched the land.

'Roo, that's nonsense,' I say. 'I could never have done half the stuff I did without you.'

'A hero never acts alone, remember?' says Lippy.

Roo doesn't look convinced. 'I suppose.'

'Anyway, where *are* you?' I ask. 'It's very dark.'

'Oh, I'm at the back of my wardrobe,' Roo replies, as though this is the most normal thing ever.

'Right. OK. Erm . . . why?'

'Because it's the only place where I get any peace,' he grumbles. 'I've got five brothers and sisters and we've all been stuck in this house for weeks now. I go to the toilet, and there's a sibling there. I try to eat my breakfast, and there's a sibling there. I try to take a nap, and there's a sibling jumping on my head. I can't do anything.'

'Ah, Roo,' I say. 'I feel your pain. I know it's hard, but –'

'I've got nothing that's just mine,' says Roo, cutting me off. 'I share my bedroom with my younger brother. My clothes were passed down from my older brother. Even my school bag belonged to someone else first. My *school bag*, guys. Sometimes I feel invisible.'

We fall into silence. I've never heard Roo say anything like this before.

'OK, well, let's get you out of there for a bit, shall we?' I declare.

Roo starts. 'Eh?'

'Come on, it'll do us all good. We'll just nip over to Fargone, talk to Teg, and then come back with some answers about Cadno and this stupid rain.'

Roo sits up. 'I'm game.'

'Excellent. Lippy?'

'All right, fine. But we might need a dinghy to get to the portal at the castle. It's bad out there.'

I grin. 'It's just a bit of rain. What harm can it do?'

'This rain could do so much harm!'

We're in the kitchen. Me, Dad, Pa, Edie and Cadno. Pa is standing by the table, arms crossed over his chest. Edie sits in her high chair, while Dad balances his phone on Cadno's belly to see if it will charge. After a few seconds, it lights up.

'Ha! It works!' he hoots.

Pa and I ignore him.

'It's just rain, Pa,' I groan.

'It's *unprecedented* rain, Charlie,' he corrects me. 'The roads have turned to rivers! And there could be flash floods! Did you think of that?'

'No, but –'

'And what if the dam bursts and you get swept away and we never see you again? I bet you didn't think of that, either? Eh? EH?!'

'All right, let's calm down with the caveman sounds,' Dad intervenes. 'The mayor said they would warn us if things got worse. And have they done that?'

Pa falters. 'No.'

'And if the dam was to burst – *which it won't*,' Dad adds hastily, 'Fargone will be safer than here, anyway. I say we let him go.'

Pa shoots Dad a glare, and his eye twitches in a way that reminds me of a robot that's about to malfunction.

'All right, fine!' he finally exclaims. 'Have it your way. You can go to Fargone –'

I punch the air in triumph.

'But I want you back by teatime. Understood?'

'Deal,' I say. 'Into Fargone, talk to Teg, come home.'

'Good,' says Pa, and I turn to go, excitement thrumming through my veins. 'We'll look after Cadno while you're gone.'

I freeze and slowly turn back. 'What?'

'Well, you can't take him out there, can you?' says Pa, nodding at the window, where the rain continues to fall torrentially. 'He might not be a firefox any more, but electricity and water don't go well together, either.'

My heart sinks. I hadn't thought of that. I dread to think what will happen to Cadno if he gets wet now he's an electrafox.

Almost as though he can understand what we're saying, Cadno starts whining. He's actually been whining a lot since he lost his flames, but these whines are more insistent.

'I'm sorry, boy, but Pa's right. It's too dangerous for you out there.'

I settle a hand on his head, feeling the hum of static prickle up my arm. Cadno leans into my touch, which is his way of pleading with me not to leave without him.

'Maybe there *is* a way for Cadno to go,' Dad says suddenly.

I look up. 'How?'

'My fellow Challinors.' He grins. 'It's time for a fashion show . . .'

'Pink really is your colour, Cadno,' I giggle.

Cadno, sitting in the middle of the living room, lets out a disgruntled sigh.

'What's wrong, boy?' asks Dad. 'Don't you like it? I think you look dashing!'

'My coat!' Edie whines. 'My coat!'

As it turns out, Cadno is a size 2–3 in toddler clothes. It took a lot of wrestling and a few electric shocks strong enough to make Dad say a word I'm not allowed to use, but we eventually managed to stuff Cadno into Edie's new raincoat. Now he's ready to brave any storm, decked out in glossy pink, covered in rainbows and looking adorable.

Cadno doesn't seem to agree. He looks thoroughly unimpressed.

'It really makes your eyes *pop*,' says Dad.

Pa nods. 'You *do* look gorgeous. All the other firefoxes are going to be so jealous of you.'

Cadno turns away and points his snout into the air, unwilling to entertain our nonsense any longer.

'Right, we're ready to go,' I say, grabbing my own coat from the bottom of the stairs. Cadno perks up when he realizes we're actually about to leave the house and starts whizzing round in circles, his entire body flashing and sparking like a light bulb that's about to explode.

'Hold still,' I say. 'All right, I'll see you later.'

'Stay away from deep bodies of water!' Pa fusses as I head for the door.

'I know.'

'And remember: into Fargone, talk to Teg, come home. Yes?'

'I *know*, Pa!'

Chapter 4

Some countries get a lot of sun. Some countries get a lot of snow. But here in Wales, we get a lot of rain. And I mean a *lot*. There are some puddles around that simply never dry up.

Still, nothing could have prepared me for what awaits us on the other side of the front door. Thick, spitting sheets, pouring from the clouds without end, as if Bryncastell is trapped beneath a gargantuan waterfall.

Everything is saturated with water. Our front lawn is now a pond, and the road beyond is a river, the

drains that are supposed to help rainwater flow away long since clogged with mushy leaves. The water doesn't have anywhere to go any more, so now it's just . . . rising.

It's bad. Worse than I'd even imagined.

I take a deep breath. 'Come on. Let's go.'

Cadno hesitates. It's ingrained in him to avoid water. You can't undo an instinct like that, so I pick him up and hold him close to my chest.

'It's all right. I've got you.'

We set off into the downpour. I know the streets of Bryncastell like the back of my hand, but the whole world has turned blurry and it's difficult to navigate when you're trying to avoid the ginormous pools that have formed everywhere.

Still, I somehow manage to get to the agreed meeting point at the base of the hill that leads up to the castle. The rest of the Adventure Squad are already there, cowering beneath a sycamore tree with their hoods drawn and their faces grim.

Well, Lippy's is grim. Roo looks like he's excited about a day out at the beach.

'Charlie!' he exclaims, grinning goofily. 'A fine day for an adventure, don't you think?'

'Erm, yes, it's just . . . lovely.'

Lippy steps forward, looking disconcerted. 'He's been like this since we got here. Awfully chirpy for somebody who would usually rather avoid danger. Who are you and what have you done with the real Roo?'

Roo glares at her. 'I've been cooped up in that house with my brothers and sisters for *three weeks*, OK? In that time, I have played Jenga sixty-seven times. I have mastered the art of face-painting. I have had to take part in three teddy-bear tea parties a day. So excuse me if I'm a little excited for a change of scene.'

'OK, fair enough,' says Lippy, then she grins at me. 'Anyway, Charlie, it's so good to see you! Are you ready to – *OhmygoshCadnoyoulooksocuuuuuteeeeeeeeeee!*'

She bounds forward, and suddenly Cadno is out of my arms and in Lippy's instead.

'You look *gorgeous*!' she informs him. 'Pink is really your colour! I've missed you, you little bundle of fire! No, wait, you're a little bundle of lightning now, aren't you?'

Lippy's eyes widen in alarm, and Cadno whines, upset by her fear. Usually, Lippy and Roo don't hesitate to scoop him up into a *cwtch*, but now she's trying to thrust him back into my arms.

He gives me sad-puppy eyes.

'Don't worry, he's not going to electrocute you,' I promise. 'It's the same as with his fire. He gets a bit . . . erm . . . *zappy* when he's angry or scared, but other than that it's just a bit of tingly static.'

Lippy laughs nervously and brings Cadno back into her chest. 'Oh, OK . . . let's try to keep him calm, then, shall we? Who's a good boy? Yes, you! *You* are the goodest boy!'

Cadno wriggles uncontrollably at this highest of compliments and licks at her face, a spark jumping from his tongue to her cheek now that he's finally getting the affection he craves. Lippy lets out a shriek of surprise.

'Argh! It feels funny!'

Roo and I chuckle, and for a moment it's as though we're not standing in the middle of a storm that could bring about the end of the world as we know it. Or the end of Bryncastell, at least.

But then a fresh curtain of rain spits through the cover provided by the tree, splattering our hoods and our faces, and we're reminded of the task at hand. Cadno whimpers and retreats into Edie's coat.

'Right,' I say, my voice grave. 'Let's make a move, then, shall we?'

The castle seems to have grown a moat, its hill now surrounded on all sides by a swollen circle of water. We surrender to the fact that we're going to get even wetter and wade our way through.

'Are you still happy about this adventure, Roo?' Lippy calls as we splash through the murky brown waters.

Roo, who has, surprisingly, taken the lead, shouts back over his shoulder, 'Couldn't be happier!'

'I just want to get to Fargone and see Blodyn and Branwen,' Lippy mutters. 'I've missed them.'

I've missed Fargone, too. That place feels like a home away from home now. Ever since I was given a sealstone of my own, we've been able to visit whenever we want – mostly on weekends, sometimes for a whole day at a time. Once or twice, Lippy and Roo have told their parents that they're coming for a sleepover at my place, when we've actually gone and stayed the night in Fargone. Dad and Pa haven't minded – they know we're safe, now that there's no threat from giant shadowdragons any more. They've even joined us a couple of times.

We've watched as Teg's Gallivant Menagerie has grown into a bustling haven for injured magical creatures. We've explored Fargone's forests and hills, and visited many of its settlements, sleepy little villages and towns where the inhabitants have treated us like royalty.

But for Lippy, the arrival of the rain and the end of our visits have proved to be even more difficult. It's been sweet seeing the way that she and Branwen have grown closer, always laughing and making each other blush. I once saw them holding hands as they walked around the palace grounds with Blodyn. I know she's desperate to see them again.

I nod in agreement. 'I hope it's not raining there, too. I'll be happy if I never see another drop ever again.'

We slosh out of the 'moat' and begin our ascent of the hill. Usually when we get to the top, we pause to take in the view of Bryncastell and the surrounding valleys. On a clear day, you can sometimes see the dam in the distance.

But not today. Today, all we can see is rain.

We cross under the portcullis and into the castle grounds, winding round until we get to our usual spot in the courtyard on the other side. The familiar curtain of ivy looks just like any other, but we know better. Behind it is a wall of stone where the veil between our world and Fargone is thinner. Where, with the help of a certain object, it's possible to open a doorway between the two.

I reach into my pocket for that object now.

'Do you have it?' asks Lippy, her eyes twinkling with excitement.

'Here it is,' I say, holding out the sealstone: a simple stone with a swirl engraved in the middle. 'Are we ready?'

'More than ever,' says Lippy.

'Get me back into Fargone right now!' says Roo.

I grin. 'Adventure Squad on tour?'

'Adventure Squad on tour!'

I turn to the ivy, hold out the sealstone and watch as the leaves ripple, stone turning to air, a breeze from another realm drifting through.

We're finally going back to Fargone.

Chapter 5

It's not raining in the queendom of Fargone.

We emerge from the portal, and we're met by the same forest as always, ancient ruins slowly being gobbled up by the moss behind us. I listen for that familiar *pitter-patter* on the canopy, the same sound I've heard pounding against our rooftop for the last three weeks, and hear nothing except gentle woodland noises: birds chirruping, critters scurrying through the undergrowth.

'Ah, it's good to be back,' says Roo, and I agree.

Now that we've left Wales and the rain behind, the tension melts from my body like thawing snow. I put Cadno on the ground and help him out of his raincoat, then we stow away our own jackets in our backpacks. The excitement is already coursing up and down his body in the form of tiny ripples of electricity. He seems to have forgotten, for a moment, about his lost fire, swept up instead by the promise of adventure.

'We're here!' Lippy squeals, and then she bursts forward, throwing her arms out as she starts twirling round like a whirligig. 'Come on, let's go find some blue sky!'

And then we're running and laughing at the same time, the forest turning to a green blur around us. Cadno barks joyfully, sparks flying from his fur as he goes. I don't ever want to stop running, but eventually we come to a glade, and the bowl of the sky opens up above us.

It's so big and bright and *blue*. I have to squint just to look at it. My eyes have got used to the gloom.

'I forgot what a clear sky looks like!' Lippy

exclaims, and then she and Roo are dancing. Cadno bounds over and prances around their feet.

'And what's that big, fiery ball thing in the sky?' I ask.

'Hmm, I can't remember what it's called,' says Roo, pausing to scratch his chin. 'It sounds like mun, or pun, or bun, or bum . . .'

'Firebum!' Lippy hoots, and then we're all doubled over with laughter.

'All hail the firebum in the sky!' we chant.

This is what happens when you're starved of sunlight and blue skies for weeks on end, I guess.

But then something passes across the sky, and we're thrust into shadow all over again.

We stop dancing.

'Hey, what happened to the firebum?' Roo scowls, glancing upward.

I bring my hand to my forehead, creating a visor, and squint. The sun has gone, replaced by a black spot that seems to be *growing*, like a blot of spilled ink.

'What is *that*?' I ask, my mouth hanging open.

'I don't know,' says Lippy, 'but it's getting bigger . . .'

She's right. But not only that, it's getting bigger *fast*. And it's heading right for us.

'Run!' cries Roo.

We bolt for the cover of the trees as a stone whistles from the sky and smashes into the ground a few metres from us, sending up a cloud of earth. We're almost thrown off our feet. A dome of electric power flashes round Cadno as his fear grows.

Another strikes just to our left, like a tiny meteorite from outer space. They start pummelling everywhere, leaving craters all over the clearing. Detritus from the giant thingumawhatsit that's hurtling down from overhead, I realize, now so big it's almost taking up the whole sky.

We reach the trees, leaping behind a felled log and peering over the top just as the humongous object collides with the earth. The impact shakes the entire world, an explosion of dust and dirt engulfing us. I close my eyes and cling to the log for dear life as the ground trembles. It's so loud it sounds like Fargone is going to split in two.

And then . . . silence. The ground stills, the dust settles, and we're left with just the echoes of the

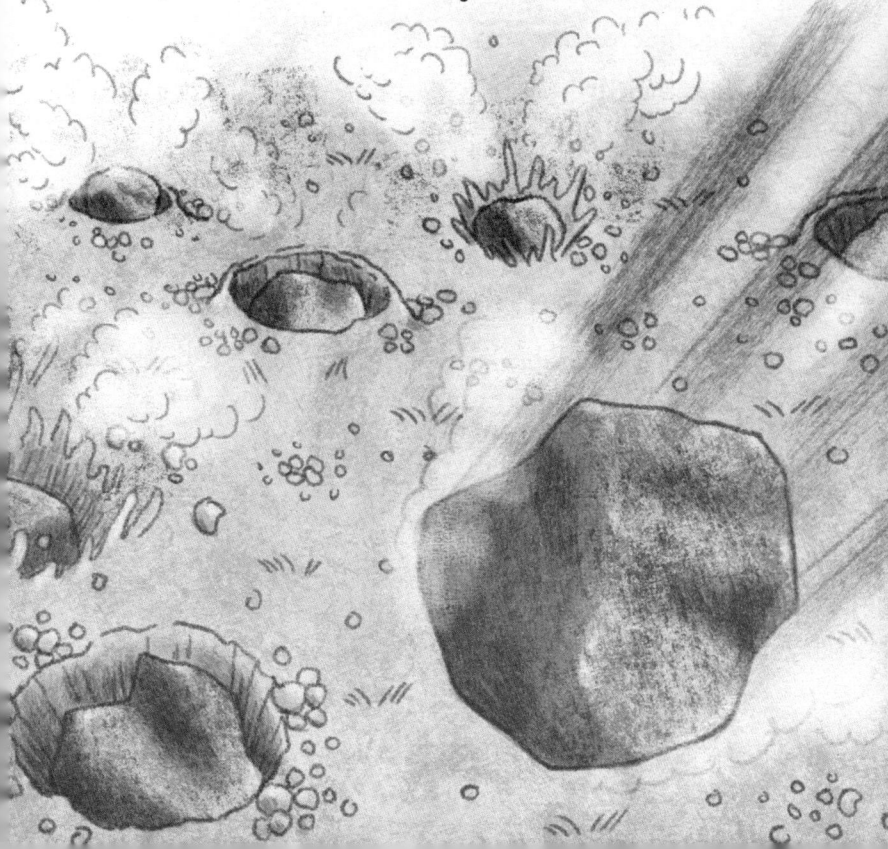

collision rattling about inside our heads and adrenaline thrumming through our veins.

'Is it safe?' comes a small voice to my right. It's Roo, his earlier eagerness suddenly diminished.

'I don't know,' I mutter. 'I think so.'

We emerge from our hiding place and creep to the margins of the clearing, where the haze of debris is just beginning to clear. A hulking form comes into focus in the centre of the glade, sitting at the bottom of a basin created by its impact.

I can hardly believe what I'm seeing.

It's . . . a *castle*. An actual castle, as real as the one on the hill in Bryncastell. It's mostly a pile of shattered stones now, mashed together with the island of earth it was built on, but chunks of wall are still intact, and narrow, rectangular windows for archers to poke their arrows through.

These are the trademark qualities of a castle if ever I've seen them. And I should know: I live in Wales, the *land* of castles.

Now, I've seen a lot of strange things since Cadno came into my life. I've seen our social worker turn into a black-eyed, many-toothed monster, witnessed an acorn grow into a fawn, and watched a fleet of firefoxes perform a dizzying dance that hypnotized a ferocious shadowdragon.

And yet none of them seems quite as strange as seeing a castle simply . . . fall from the heavens.

'Guys, I think I preferred it when there was only water falling from the sky,' says Roo, taking very careful steps backwards, in the direction we came from. 'Shall we . . . er, y'know, go home now?'

'You've changed your tune,' I say pointedly. 'No way. This is too weird, even by Fargone's standards. Castles don't just fall out of nowhere. Something is going on, and we need to find out what.'

Roo groans. 'And there was me hoping for a simple, straightforward adventure. Why are there always things that nearly kill us?'

'Charlie's right,' says Lippy, stepping forward with a determined look on her face. 'We didn't sign up for a quiet life, did we?'

'Erm, I did,' says Roo, putting his hand up. 'I literally wanted peace and quiet, away from my siblings –'

'You were the one who wanted to get out of Bryncastell so bad,' I say. 'Well, now we're out. And it looks like the Adventure Squad has a job to do. First things first, we need to find out what's going on.'

'B-but how can we do that?' Roo stammers.

A smile grows on my lips. 'Oh, I think I know somebody who can help. Cadno, do your magic.'

Cadno sits bolt upright and throws his head back, unleashing a long, other-worldly call that ripples through the dell and into the air.

When he's done, the silence returns.

'What now?' asks Roo.

'Same as usual,' I say. 'We wait.'

Chapter 6

'I've waited less time for a bus,' Roo says, after about twenty minutes. 'A bus being driven by my *nan*.'

We're back at our log, waiting as the minutes tick by. Life has returned to the forest once again, the foliage around us buzzing with energy.

'She'll be here!' Lippy snaps. 'She never lets us down, does she?'

Roo goes quiet, and Lippy stares into the forest, her face alert. But Roo does have a point – she never usually takes this long.

'Maybe something is up,' I say.

'*No*. She'll be here. I know she will –'

Cadno starts barking, sending a flurry of sparks into the air. Sure enough, I can hear twigs snapping as something approaches. And then the trees part and a familiar creature emerges.

I suck in a breath.

It's Blodyn the floradoe, but not the Blodyn I remember. Blodyn is usually a lush, leafy green, with specks of emerald worked through her fur and glistening threads of gossamer strung between her antlers.

This Blodyn is white, the colour of untouched snow, and instead of flowers adorning her horns, there are webs of frost, and a single icicle dangling from the topmost antler.

She steps into the clearing, her movements stiff and awkward, like she's trying not to touch anything.

Lippy gasps and rushes forward, but the floradoe rears up, warding her off. Our friend pauses, and I watch in dreadful fascination as ice spreads out across the grass from Blodyn's hoofs, turning every blade within a metre white and crispy.

'B-Blodyn,' Lippy stutters. 'What's happened to you?'

Blodyn lets out a mournful sound and Cadno yaps, sending up a fresh shower of electric sparks. Blodyn blinks in surprise, and then continues wailing. It's almost like they're having a chat, I think – and that's when I realize.

'She's switched, too,' I whisper, 'just like Cadno has! She's not a floradoe any more! Now she's a . . . erm, a . . .'

'A *frost*doe,' Lippy puts in.

'They don't look very happy,' says Roo.

He's right: their heads are bowed and they're both making sad sounds. It's as if they're having a good moan together.

'But what's happening?' asks Lippy, her voice pained. 'Why are their powers switching? Blodyn, just let me come to you. I promise it will be OK.'

At first, Blodyn retreats, but when it becomes clear that Lippy isn't going to give up, she relents and stays still. Lippy comes to stand next to her and reaches out with a hand that's ever-so-slightly trembling to touch her fur.

'She's freezing,' says Lippy in astonishment. 'It's like she's made out of ice – argh!'

She squeals and pulls her hand away, lifting her finger to show us. The tip is white and encased in frost. She gives her hand a shake, sending flakes of ice everywhere.

'Oh, Blodyn!' she laments. 'What's happened? All I want to do is hug you, and I can't!'

Blodyn grunts in agreement and hangs her head, while Cadno does the same, both of them visibly distressed at having lost their original powers.

'So we've got a firefox that's now an electrafox, and a floradoe that's now a frostdoe,' I say. 'This gets worse and worse.'

'You're right,' says Lippy. 'And we know where we need to go.'

Roo and I nod.

'Blodyn?' asks Lippy.

The deer looks up.

'Can you take us to the Gallivant Menagerie?'

Blodyn sets her mouth in a determined line, as though she's glad to have been asked for something she knows how to do. She sends a call into the woods, and this time it takes less than a minute for two other deer to appear through the trees.

'Our noble steeds have arrived!' Lippy declares. 'Good job, Blods.'

We take a deer each, with Lippy clambering aboard Blodyn. Their bond is unshakably strong now, a bit like mine and Cadno's, and Lippy manages to calm Blodyn enough that she can control her temperature, so that Blodyn doesn't turn Lippy into a block of ice when she takes her mount.

'Are we ready?' Lippy asks.

'Ready,' I say. Roo mumbles something incoherent.

'Right. Hold on tight. Next stop, the Gallivant Menagerie!'

Every time we come to Fargone, the Gallivant Menagerie has moved somewhere new. Teg started the enterprise when he returned to Fargone after our run-in with the Grendilock: a safe place for magical creatures to take shelter or recover from illness or injury; a roaming sanctuary. Sometimes it's tucked away in the forest, other times it's nestled on the shores of crystal-blue lakes in the mountains. Teg has managed to grow it from just a few carriages into a whole wagon train that rattles through the wilds to every corner of Fargone.

Usually when we arrive, we find the camp in some state of celebration or fun. Even if Teg is tending to an animal that's unwell, there's always a bunch of other beasts getting up to mischief or having a party. Today, however, we find it in complete turmoil.

It's in the middle of a field, and as we approach, I can hear shouting, barking and roaring.

None of them are happy sounds.

'What's going on?' I wonder aloud as we round the back of a carriage – and freeze as three balls of fire drift into our path. As in *actual* baubles of flaming lava floating through the air. It's a near miss for my eyebrows. I can feel the searing heat, even as the orbs seem to *pop*, a bit like –

'Fire bubbles!' Lippy cries. 'The flying seahorses!'

We wait for the last of the fire bubbles to float by and then we turn the corner, into the main circle of the camp.

What we find is complete and utter bedlam.

Lippy was right about the flying seahorses: there they are, flitting about as they always do, except instead of spouting regular bubbles from their noses, they're jetting out those fire bubbles that almost burned our faces off.

The rest of the camp's residents are in an equal state of confusion. The stone teddy bear (a rockabear, according to Teg), who famously crushed one of my pa's most beloved mugs in our garden, is barely recognizable. Instead of stone, he's now made from moss, with mushrooms sprouting from his body and a giant red toadstool atop his head. He plods around miserably, fresh fungi blooming from whatever he touches.

Then I spot Kevin the drill marten, one of Teg's closest companions, whose drill-nose usually allows him to burrow deep under the ground. Now his drill has been replaced by a mechanism that looks a bit like a hairdryer. It's blowing with such force that poor Kevin is rocketing around in the air, like a hosepipe out of control.

And there, running after him with his arms out, is none other than Teg himself.

He, at least, looks the same as when we last saw him, although I've never seen him so panicked.

'I've got you, Kevin!' he shouts. 'Don't worry, I won't let you fall!'

'Teg!' I call.

Our friend turns, spots us and stops in his tracks, his face lighting up.

'What are you folks doing here?' he says, gawping.

Then there's a thud behind him as Kevin crashes to the ground, his airstream turned off.

'Kevin!' Teg scoops up his friend, who looks a bit stunned. 'You had to wait until I went and turned my back, didn't you?'

'Teg, what's going on?'

'Shh, Kevin, it's OK, it's OK,' Teg says soothingly, without looking up. 'I'm going to need some bandages. Albie, where are you? Oh, where's he hiding now? Albie, come out, you cowardly snabbit!'

He's met with silence – or at least silence from Albanact the snabbit. The rest of the camp continues to fall apart around us.

'Albanact, as the Chief of the Gallivant Menagerie, aka *your boss*,' Teg snarls menacingly, 'I command you to stop neglecting your duties as my Deputy Camp Supervisor and come out at once, forthwith!'

'*Deputy Camp Supervisor*,' whispers Roo. 'Somebody's had a promotion.'

A few seconds pass, and then a clump of grass near the middle of the circle that the camp has formed begins to shudder. I hear the muffled sound of huffing and puffing from below, and then the clump lifts into the air with Albanact the snabbit underneath it, looking grumpier than usual.

'Neglecting my duties,' he mutters, dusting earth off himself as he waddles over. 'How very dare he. He knows how seriously I take my role . . .'

'Oh, so you just happened to be hiding underground?' Teg hisses. 'Nothing to do with avoiding the chaos all around us?'

'The mud is good for my shell,' retorts Albie. 'You'll see! In a few minutes, I'll be positively sparkling.'

'Well, let's hope you can clean up your act as well, because at the moment you're heading for the sack.'

Albie gasps. 'You would never.'

Teg glares at him. 'Try me. The whole camp is falling apart and you've done nothing but –'

'Guys, guys, guys!' I say, stepping forward. 'Can you please tell us what's going on?'

Teg looks abashed. 'I'm sorry. It's just . . . well, it's been a very testing day. We –' He stops short, his gaze finally landing on Cadno, who's giving off anxious electric sparks, and Blodyn, who seems to be generating a miniature blizzard.

'Oh dear,' he says. 'This isn't just a casual visit, is it?'

We shake our heads.

Teg takes a deep breath. 'All right. Let's go to the hospital carriage. Albie, fetch my compendium and meet us there.'

Chapter 7

The hospital carriage is painted white, with a red stripe round the middle. Inside, it looks a bit like an ambulance, if an ambulance was made from wood. There's a bed on wheels, shelves packed with jars of medicinal herbs and ointments, and some cages with tiny, resting inhabitants. Occupying one cage is something that looks like a teeny, fluffy elephant, a harsh, screeching note humming out of its trunk as it sleeps, while a large perch dangling from the ceiling has a pair of long, sausagey creatures covered in brown fur sitting on it, their faces hidden as they nuzzle into each other.

'What are they?' asks Roo, pointing.

Teg casts a sad glance upward. 'Oh, those are the wotters. Water-type otter creatures. Or at least they *were* wotters before all this chaos started. They used to be able to summon whirlpools, but now they can't do anything watery and have instead started flying.'

'Teg, what's going on?' I ask again.

He sets Kevin down on the wheelie bed, just as Albanact enters carrying a giant bundle of paper clumsily bound with string.

'Thank you, Albie,' says Teg, taking it and setting it down on a counter with a *thump*. He pulls a roll of bandages from a drawer and starts wrapping Kevin's new hairdryer snout, which does look a bit swollen from his fall.

'So we've got a fire type who's switched to an electric type,' says Teg as he works, 'a plant type who's switched to an ice type, and a bunch of other types that have switched, too. Interesting.'

'Teg,' I press, 'what are you talking about?'

'I'm getting to it,' he says, holding up a finger. 'Just thinking out loud for a second.'

He finishes patching up Kevin's snout, which now looks sort of mummified, then fetches the tome from the counter.

'After you defeated Draig, if you remember, Branwen offered to make me Fargone's first ever official Magical Creatures Liaison Officer,' says Teg, with an air of pride. 'In the end I decided to accept the post, and one of my first undertakings was to start compiling the first ever encyclopaedia of magical creatures. This is the *Fargone Compendium of Magical Creatures*.' He casts us a meek glance. 'It's a working title.'

He opens the manuscript and starts leafing through. Each page is dedicated to a magical creature, including a sketch and a written description of its appearance, its diet, its habitat, and how best to approach it (or to leave it well alone). Among the entries I spot a page for the firefox, another for the floradoe, and others for the wotter, the rockabear and the spidergong, the stretchmunk and the twisterantula – although we've never come across the latter and, judging from the illustration, I don't particularly want to.

'Every new creature I met, I would observe it and write down what I saw. After a while, I noticed that each magical creature displayed a certain type of magic. The firefox, for example, uses fire magic; the floradoe, plant magic.'

Teg points to the corner of the firefox page, where he has drawn a little circle with a flame inside. Next to it are the words *Fire Type*. He turns to Blodyn's entry, where there's another circle in the corner with a flower inside, and the words *Plant Type* scribbled next to it.

'I started developing something that I'm calling the Theory of Magical Disciplines in Fargone's Fauna,' Teg goes on.

'Bit of a mouthful, isn't it?' says Roo.

'It makes me sound clever,' says Teg curtly.

'Can't argue with that. Go on.'

'The Theory of Magical Disciplines in Fargone's Fauna states that each magical creature has a discipline, or type,' says Teg. 'I've observed loads of types so far. There's fire, plant, air, water, electric, ice, earth, bug, and mysterious ones like shadow, music and mystic.'

'Mystic?' I frown.

'Yep, tricky to define, that one,' says Teg. 'But mystic-type creatures can do inexplicable things, like move objects with their minds, or do dream magic, or . . . Take the grizzlarth, for example! The grizzlarth is a mystic type. He can make people and animals around him fall into a deep sleep.' His expression sinks. 'Or at least he used to.'

'Where is the grizzlarth?' asks Lippy. 'I haven't seen him since we arrived.'

'Yeah, he's like that at the moment,' Teg grumbles. 'He's got this new thing where he just randomly – AAAAAARGH!'

Just then, the grizzlarth appears behind Teg as though out of thin air. His frame is now so huge that his head touches the ceiling, the entire carriage rocking around us. The wotters, who until now have been asleep, leap from their perch and soar over to the corner, where they cast the grizzlarth disgruntled looks and start twirling round each other in a graceful dance.

'Hey, buddy!' I grin, and the grizzlarth holds up a big, fluffy paw in greeting. 'That was new! Did he just . . . erm, *teleport*?'

'Everything is new,' Teg groans as the grizzlarth lumbers round him, squeezing us all into the tiny space like a bunch of sardines. 'I can't keep up with anything any more. All the animals have switched types, and I don't know why.'

'So the grizzlarth doesn't have sleep powers any more,' says Lippy. 'Instead, he can teleport?'

The grizzlarth pulls a face, like he thinks we're all a bit *twp*. Unlike some of the other animals, the grizzlarth's appearance is mostly the same as the last time we saw him. He's still covered in the same purple fur; it's just the swirl on his belly that has changed, the one he used to hypnotize people.

Now, in its place, is what looks like a clock face.

'Mate,' Teg grunts to the grizzlarth. He's pressed up against the bear's belly, and it looks like he's about

to disappear into its fur. 'Do you mind? It's a bit cramped in here as it is.'

The grizzlarth rolls his eyes and then disappears once again. Teg lets out a breath of relief.

'Yeah, so everything is completely messed up and I don't know why,' he says, closing the compendium with an air of defeat. Now that the grizzlarth has gone, the wotters glide down from the ceiling and re-settle on their perch. It swings gently under their weight as they curl up round each other and fall asleep again.

'Are the wotters OK, Teg?' asks Roo.

Teg, who was staring hopelessly into the distance, blinks. 'Wha– Oh yes. I mean, they don't have a physical sickness.'

'What do you mean?' I say.

'Their ailment is more to do with the mind,' Teg explains. 'These wotters are both female, and they love each other dearly. They don't leave each other's side. But lately, they've been very sad . . . I think it's because they want a baby, but, of course, they can't produce young because they're both female.'

'Those poor wotters!' Lippy cries. 'I'm sure they'd make amazing mums.'

'I think so, too,' says Teg, nodding sadly. 'I keep them in here for now, away from the chaos of the camp. Speaking of which . . . To summarize, we have a firefox who's now an electrafox . . .'

Cadno gives an unhappy zap on the floor.

'A floradoe who's now a frostdoe . . .'

Blodyn snorts miserably, sending a puff of fresh snowflakes into the air.

'And a whole bunch of other magical creatures who've got their types confused,' Teg finishes.

'What about you, Albanact?' asks Lippy. 'You're still a snabbit, aren't you?'

Albanact is about to open his mouth to answer, but Teg bursts out laughing. The snabbit's face settles into a glare. 'And what, may I ask, is so funny?'

'Oh, nothing. It's just . . . well, there's not much magical about snabbits, is there? You can't get your powers confused if you don't have any!'

'I'll have you know I come from a long line of talented snabbits,' Albie says haughtily. 'We have gifts few people understand!'

'Mmm-hmm, sure,' says Teg, then covers his mouth with his hand and whispers to me: 'Shame he couldn't have had a personality transplant. He's still as grumpy as ever.'

'I heard that!'

'I'm just joking, Albie.'

'So what are we going to do?' asks Roo. 'Everything is a mess. Is there anything we can do to help? Maybe I could –'

'No!' Teg practically shouts, and Roo winces. Teg smiles gingerly. 'I mean, er . . . no, thank you, Roo, although that is very kind of you to offer.'

'What's the problem?' Roo frowns, glancing from Teg, to me, to Lippy.

Teg gazes wearily at us. 'Well . . . it's just, I mean . . .' he starts, and then he takes a deep breath. 'Oh, fine. No offence, Roo, but it's just that you're not exactly . . . erm . . . *efficient*, are you?'

Roo crosses his arms over his chest. 'What's that supposed to mean?'

'Do you remember last time you visited?' says Teg. 'One of the seahorses flew down a burrow and you went to fetch it, only you got your head stuck instead.'

Roo's expression falls. 'Yes, I remember.'

'And there was that time –'

'Yeah, all right!' Roo interrupts, looking crestfallen. 'You've made your point. I'm useless.'

'You are not useless, Roo!' says Lippy. 'You're just . . . good at other things.'

Roo narrows his eyes. 'Oh yeah, like what?'

Lippy looks uncomfortable, but then Teg sweeps in.

'Anyway, no time to waste! As Fargone's official Magical Creatures Liaison Officer, I have thought *long and hard* about this situation –'

'It only started this morning,' says Albanact.

'I have thought long and hard *since this morning*,' Teg says, shooting Albanact a glare, 'and I have reached the conclusion . . . that I have absolutely no idea what to do.'

My mouth drops open. 'What?'

Teg shrugs. 'Sorry.'

'Then what do you suggest?' asks Lippy.

'I suggest a trip to see my boss.'

'Your *boss*?'

'Indeed,' says Teg, with a smile. 'It's time to pay a visit to the queen.'

Chapter 8

Lippy can't get going fast enough.

'Come on!' she sings. 'We can't keep the queen waiting!'

'How can we keep her waiting when she doesn't even know we're coming?' Roo groans.

'She'll be wondering where we are!' Lippy snaps. 'She hasn't seen us for weeks. Now, come on.'

The palace is only a few hours away from where the menagerie is currently parked, but it's a lot of work getting it ready to do its titular gallivanting. We have to make sure everything is strapped in, so nothing falls out when we go over bumps, and that all the animals are settled comfortably in their beds, pens and homes – which is tough when they're all so shaken up by their power changes. I almost lose my fringe trying to get the fiery seahorses back into their tank.

Finally, we're ready. We join Teg on the driving bench of the leading carriage, Kevin the hairdryer marten draped over his neck. Teg grabs the reins of a team of six (thankfully non-magical) horses, and off we go.

The road is smooth, and though Lippy hums excitedly, Roo is quiet the entire way. I think I know what's bothering him, because he keeps casting disheartened glances at Cadno, who's sitting on my lap, and at Blodyn, who's sitting on the carriage roof behind Lippy, her head resting adoringly on her shoulder.

'You OK, Roo?' I ask, and he looks up.

'What? Oh yeah. I'm fine.'

But I don't believe him.

The countryside rolls by in a beautiful carousel of green. We pass patchwork fields and glistening ponds and babbling creeks.

'Much better weather than in Wales,' Lippy trills.

'You say it's been raining for a few weeks there?' asks Teg, and the three of us nod.

'Hmm, I wonder . . .' he says, more to himself than to anybody else.

'What?' I say.

'You might be right that the rain in Wales and what's happening here in Fargone are connected somehow. You see, it's not just the animals that have started acting strangely . . . Oh, dear me.'

We round a corner and come across a scene of utter devastation.

It's a ruined village. Stone cottages with thatched roofs, except they've completely disintegrated. They're sitting atop mounds of crumbling earth, a bit like the castle that fell out of the sky earlier.

'This is exactly what I'm talking about,' says Teg, with an air of sadness.

'Did these houses fall from the sky as well?' I exclaim.

Teg blinks at me in astonishment. 'How do you know that?'

'Oh, just after we arrived through the portal, a castle fell out of the sky and nearly squished us,' says Roo casually, like we're talking about what to have for tea.

'What? Forgot to mention that one, did you?'

'Well, there was quite a lot going on when we arrived at camp,' says Lippy, gesturing at Blodyn, who's being followed by a gentle snowstorm. Looking a bit miffed that flakes keep landing on him, Kevin points his snout at her and turns his air blast on, sending them blowing in the other direction.

'Fair enough. OK, well, yes. Scenes like this are becoming more common. Villages falling from the sky left, right and centre.'

'Hang on, hang on,' says Roo. 'Why are the villages up there in the first place?'

'What do you mean?' Teg frowns. 'Don't you have sky villages in Wales?'

'Erm, nope,' says Lippy. 'Our villages tend to stay firmly on the ground.'

'That's so weird,' Teg replies. 'A few centuries ago, as the population of Talarwen was growing, the king decided to flood one of the valleys to make a reservoir. Trouble was, the closest valley had a bunch of villages in it. So instead of just drowning them, he sent them up into the sky instead. There's a whole town up there now, although it seems to have started drifting all over the place. It's called Cantre'r Awyr.'

He points up at the sky, where a patch of cloud is beginning to clear. Framed in the window it creates is a dark, blob-like shape. But then the sun catches it, and I gasp.

The dark shape is simply a floating earthy underbelly. Sitting atop it is a tower made from colourful bricks, with a twisting spire at the top that sparkles like rainbow glass. It's an island suspended above the clouds, and there, connecting it to another island, is a bridge. And another, and another, making up a whole network of hovering buildings.

'Cantre'r Awyr,' I whisper. 'That ... sounds familiar.'

'That's because it sounds like Cantre'r Gwaelod that we've been learning about in school!' Lippy exclaims. 'The towns that got drowned by the sea, remember?'

She's right! Cantre'r Gwaelod, the communities that were swallowed up by the ocean. And here, in Fargone, they have Cantre'r Awyr, the communities that were rescued from a watery fate. I'm struck once again by the similarities between Wales and Fargone. Sometimes it feels as though the two countries are holding mirrors up to each other.

'*Amazing*,' I say. 'How does it stay up there?'

'Starswans,' Teg explains. 'They spend their whole lives gliding above the clouds. They can make things float with their minds. A true mystic type if ever I've seen one. Or, at least, they used to be. The starswans' powers must be getting muddled, too. Cantre'r Awyr is usually north of here, but it's drifted. That's why there are ruins dotted all over the place. Some of the buildings float down gently, but most of them just drop like a stone.'

He points again, and I notice gaps where some of the bridges have been broken as the sky town slowly falls apart.

'Let's keep going, shall we?' says Teg. 'The sooner we get to Queen Branwen, the sooner we can hopefully get some answers.'

But we've only travelled a few more miles before we stumble across another scene of destruction. This time, it's not in the form of fallen buildings but, rather, great chasms gouged into the earth. There are lots of them, all in a line, cutting across the countryside like somebody has attacked Fargone with a giant hole-punch.

'Uh-oh,' says Teg. 'This isn't good.'

'What do you – Argh! Cadno!' I cry out when a jolt of electricity travels up my arms. Cadno is standing on my lap with his hackles raised, a growl working up from his belly and bright sparks flashing from his fur. He turns when he hears me and hangs his head, his power quickly diminishing.

'It's all right. Just please be a bit more careful next time, OK?' I comfort him, although my fingers feel slightly numb. I think I preferred his fire.

'These aren't just random holes in the ground,' says Teg darkly.

'Then what are they?' asks Lippy.

'They're footsteps,' says Teg.

Sure enough, the craters *do* have a sort of foot shape – oval, wider at one end and narrowing in the middle.

'*Footsteps!*' Roo exclaims. 'Of course! What else would they be? Don't tell me there are still dinosaurs in Fargone. Honestly, it wouldn't surprise me.'

'I have no idea what a dinosaur is.' Teg scowls. 'But no . . . there's only one thing capable of leaving footsteps this big.'

'What is it?' I ask.

'A giant,' says Teg.

'A *giant*?' Lippy and I repeat together. Wales has a rich history of giant mythology. Mountains that giants have used as seats to gaze at the stars; giants who have lain down and transformed into hills, leaving craggy outcrops that look like faces turned to the sky.

'Oh, a giant,' Roo carries on. 'How lovely. Just when this country can't get any more preposterous, it does.'

Teg ignores him. He casts a glance over his shoulder, back in the direction that the enormous footsteps seem to have come from. I can see mountains in the distance, swirling with dark clouds that look like they're about to get snagged on the peaks.

'We haven't seen a giant in Fargone for centuries,' Teg mutters. 'Not since . . .'

'Since when?' I prod, but Teg doesn't answer. He's directed his attention to the sky, like he might find some answers there, but then his eyes widen.

'Grumbling grizzlarths,' he mutters, and we follow his gaze to the clouds.

At first, I can't see what he's looking at. But then I spot them: a formation of moving dots, like a line of ants crawling across the heavens. I can't tell what they are, but there are dozens of them. *Hundreds*, even, all of them heading in the same direction – the same direction as the footsteps.

'What are those?' I gawp.

'Crafancs,' Teg mutters. 'Oh dear, this is not good . . .'

'Crafancs?' asks Roo.

'They're a sort of water monster,' explains Teg. 'Look a bit like beavers, except far more menacing.'

Roo shudders. 'Urgh, they sound hideous.'

'When people from villages near a lake go missing, it's said it's the crafancs dragging them down into the depths to eat them.'

Our mouths drop open, horrified.

'And it looks like they're not water types any more, either. They're *air* types. They've left their lakes and now they're following the giant footsteps from the sky . . .'

'What's happening, Teg?' I say, unable to tear my eyes from the crafancs. They're so high I can't make

out many details, but I can definitely see oar-like tails and sharp, pointed spines.

'Magical creatures getting their powers mixed up; a giant on the move from the lands beyond the mountains; Cantre'r Awyr falling from the sky; and never-ending rain in Wales,' Teg lists. 'This is bad. Very bad. Come on. We must get to the palace. Something terrible is happening.'

'What else is new?' says Roo under his breath.

Chapter 9

Considering the palace has a colossal front door, the bell is teeny, the size of a doorbell you'd find outside a regular house in Wales.

Teg presses it and we listen to the chirpy melody tinkling away on the other side. After a moment, the door opens with a creak and a boy appears, his dark hair scraped back into a long braid. He looks us up and down, then lets out a yawn.

The Adventure Squad don't often get this reaction in Fargone. Since we defeated Draig, there have been statues of the three of us popping up everywhere, and we can hardly walk through a village square without being mobbed by admirers. It was fun for a while but then got kind of embarrassing.

It's weird seeing yourself in statue form, looking far more heroic than you've ever actually felt. I'm usually wearing some sort of armour, with my eyebrows carved into a look of noble determination that my real eyebrows can't do (believe me, I've tried – Roo told me I looked like I was trying to hold in a fart).

The fuss is a bit much for Roo, especially the statues and the tapestries. Lippy and I are always depicted with our animal companions – me with Cadno posed valiantly at my feet, and Lippy with a hand on Blodyn's back – while Roo just sort of stands there looking a bit . . . lost.

This boy, however, looks entirely unimpressed by us. He doesn't even blink at the sight of Cadno and Blodyn with their switched powers. In fact, he looks like he'd rather be anywhere else but here.

'We've come to see the queen,' says Teg.

'Tell her Lippy is here!' Lippy grins.

'Excuse me, I'm not your servant – or the queen's, for that matter,' the boy drawls, leaning against the door frame with his arms crossed. 'Besides, Branwen the Boring is occupied at the moment –'

'Occupied with what?' Lippy scowls. 'She can't be too occupied to see us.'

The boy smiles mockingly. 'I'm afraid it's a matter of the utmost importance.'

'Nothing is more important than what we've got to tell her,' I say firmly.

The boy must register the seriousness in my voice, because he rolls his eyes and kicks the door open.

'All right, follow me,' he calls over his shoulder as he stalks away. I notice then that he's wearing expensive-looking clothes. I don't think he's a servant.

'You lot are always so dramatic. Honestly, I've only just got back from my own travels and I'm already being bossed around.'

A very grumpy soldier.

'Who *is* that?' Roo whispers to me as we all shuffle inside.

'Beats me,' I mutter. 'But he's definitely got a dragon in his dungeon.'

The Queen of Fargone is sitting on a stool in the middle of the cavernous Great Hall, with a velvet curtain strung up behind her. She's wearing a flowing scarlet cloak and in her hand is a golden sceptre. Next to her is a small table piled high with fruit, and on her lap is a poodle with fur so finely puffed up it looks like its mum was a cloud.

In front of her stands a huge canvas propped on an easel, and a man with a tiny paintbrush in one hand and a wooden palette in the other. On the canvas is a painting of the queen exactly as she appears now – majestic, splendid and . . . bored.

The grumpy boy leads us across the hall. 'There's somebody here to see you, cuz.'

Roo, Lippy and I exchange astonished glances. *Cuz?!* Clearly he's not a soldier, after all . . .

Branwen looks up, and her face illuminates with joy. 'Oh my gosh!'

She makes to bounce off the stool, but the artist hisses.

'Your Majesty, I beg of you, please stay still. Capturing the essence of your spirit is difficult enough without you moving around all the time.'

Branwen looks pained, like she's having to use physical might to keep herself seated.

'But I've already sat for a hundred of these portraits!'

From her lap, the cloud-poodle starts to yap at us. Cadno's hackles rise, warning sparks flickering across his fur.

'Hush, Selsig!' Branwen says, patting the dog, then returns her attention to us, trying to keep her face still while

simultaneously attempting to fight off a grin. 'What are you all doing here?'

'They said they had something important to tell you, blah, blah, blah,' says the young man, through a yawn.

'Thanks, Effy. I'll take it from here.'

The boy – Effy – curls his lip in disgust. 'Don't call me that.'

He marches off, pausing to study the painting over the artist's shoulder. 'You need to work on her ears. They're *much* bigger in real life.'

Branwen gasps. 'I heard that!'

Effy gives a smug smirk. 'See? I'm sure it will really help you *capture the essence of her spirit.*'

'Sorry about him,' Branwen grumbles as the boy saunters out. 'That's my cousin, Prince Efnisien. My aunties sent him here to learn the rules of court but, to be honest, he's doing my head in. He thinks he's better than everybody. Talks to the servants like they're rubbish! And he said the Grendilock was cute. Can you believe that?'

I stop myself from smiling at the Queen of Fargone saying *doing my head in*, a phrase she's clearly picked up from Lippy. She'd fit right in at school in Wales, I reckon.

'He's never liked me since I beat him at archery when we were little,' says Branwen. 'He's not stopped practising since; always saying he wants a rematch. Everything's a competition with him. And then I became queen, and now it's like he thinks he could do a better job of running the country.' She snorts. 'I'd like to see him try! He's just a spoilt brat who's upset because he's not on the throne.'

'It's so good to see you,' says Lippy. 'You look beautiful.'

A happy glow spreads across Branwen's cheeks. 'Awh, thanks, Lippy. It's good to see you, too. I've missed you!'

'There it is! The essence of your spirit!' the artist cries, clicking his fingers. He turns to Lippy. 'Can you make her do that glowy thing with her face again? I've never seen her look so happy.'

This time, it's Lippy's turn to blush.

'What are you doing, Branwen?' I ask.

'Oh, just being the queen,' she mumbles. 'I swear, all I ever do is pose for royal portraits and tapestry weavings. Do you know how hard it is to sit for hours on end and not even be allowed to scratch an itch or – Wait, what's happened to Cadno and Blodyn?'

Selsig the cloud-poodle has started barking again, and this time Cadno can't stop the sparks of electricity from dancing across his fur. Frost begins to crystallize at the base of Blodyn's hoofs.

'Oh, be quiet, Selsig!' Branwen admonishes him. 'Honestly, what do you think you're going to do against a firefox and a floradoe?'

Selsig settles down with a resentful whimper.

'Well, that's kinda the thing,' I say. 'They're not really a firefox or a floradoe any more.'

'What?'

'With all due respect, Your Majesty,' says Teg, dipping into a bow, 'we need to talk.'

'Hmm. Yes, you're right,' replies Branwen. 'Rhodri, I think it's time I took a break. My back is getting quite stiff.'

The artist sets down his brush. 'Very well, Your Majesty.'

Branwen stands, shrugs off her cloak and drapes it over the stool. She sets down her sceptre, then removes the crown from her head – the same one we stole from this very palace to distract the gold-loving Draig on our last adventure.

'Thank goodness for that,' she says, and hurries over to wrap her arms round Lippy and plant a kiss on her cheek. 'I was melting under there. Now, come on. Let me take you to the Map Room.'

Chapter 10

The Map Room is exactly what it sounds like: a big room with a three-dimensional map of Fargone mounted on a table in the middle, with floor-to-ceiling windows that overlook the sprawling capital city, Talarwen, and Fargone beyond.

'Wow,' I say in awe. 'What do you use this room for?'

'Oh, just to talk and plan and stuff,' Branwen replies. 'Now, tell me what's happening.'

My friends all look at me expectantly, so I launch into an account of everything that's happened so far: the endless rain in Wales, Cadno and Blodyn changing powers, Cantre'r Awyr falling, the giant footsteps, and the crafancs following them from the sky.

By the time I'm finished, Branwen looks a bit green. She doesn't get time to reply, however, because at that very moment the door to the Map Room bursts open, and a young girl with flushed cheeks comes running through, clasping a scroll.

'Your Majesty,' she pants, coming to a standstill before us.

'What's wrong, Anwen?' asks Branwen.

'I beg your pardon for interrupting, Your Majesty, but this message has arrived for you. The messenger would have been here much sooner if it wasn't for the arrow wound.'

Branwen's jaw tightens. She takes the scroll from the girl with a nod of gratitude, then unfurls it. We wait as her eyes race across it.

'Oh dear,' she finally says.

'What's happened?' I ask.

Branwen grips the back of a chair for balance. 'I think I need to sit down. This is an awful lot to process.'

She takes a seat and a deep breath. 'It would seem that the Cariad has been stolen from its keep.'

Teg gasps.

'The *what* has been stolen from its *what*?' Lippy echoes.

But Branwen isn't done. 'And it was stolen by none other than Gawr himself.'

Teg gasps again, this time even louder.

I put a hand up. 'OK, hold on a sec. Can somebody please explain what's going on? What's the Cariad? Who's Gawr?'

'The Cariad is the heart of Fargone,' says Teg. 'An ancient artefact that was created to keep the magic of the land in balance, by a race of talented inventors, long since forgotten. For centuries, it's been guarded in a mountain keep. If it's been stolen, that explains everything!'

'No, it doesn't,' says Roo. 'Fargone newbies here, remember?'

'I keep forgetting you don't know our history,' says Teg.

'All right, gather round,' says Branwen, beckoning us closer. 'It's story time. You see, a long time ago, Fargone was a far less safe place than it is now –'

Roo snorts, and Branwen shoots him a glare. We all sit round the map table, Cadno on my lap, Blodyn standing at Lippy's shoulder, and Kevin draped over Teg's.

'As I was saying, back when the world was young, Fargone was a playground for monsters. And worst among them were the giants. They were ruled by the nastiest, biggest of them all. His name was Gawr. The stories say that he used to flatten a village every morning just for fun, and bite the peaks from mountains.'

'Sounds like a lovely chap,' says Roo.

'But one day,' Branwen goes on, 'as it has often done throughout history, Fargone presented us with a hero. This time, it came in the form of the sunlion.'

'*Sunlion?*' I whisper.

Branwen nods. 'A mighty beast with the face and front body of a lion, and the wings and back talons of an eagle. His name is Llew.'

'Llew,' says Lippy, turning the word over in her mouth. Her face lights up. 'That's the Welsh word for *lion*!'

She's right! I'm struck once again by the similarities between Fargone and Wales; how our language has somehow managed to leak through the veil between our dimensions, and even our histories and mythologies seem entwined, like with the story of Cantre'r Awyr – two lost settlements, one in each country.

'Llew is strengthened by the power of the sun, and at full strength he can produce a hyperbeam – a beam of pure sun energy. Nothing can stand against it.'

'Wow,' we all say in unison.

'Indeed. The sunlion rose over the top of the mountains and, using his hyperbeam, managed to defeat Gawr once and for all. Or, at least, sort of.'

'What do you mean, *sort of*?' asks Roo.

Branwen grimaces. 'Well, Llew's hyperbeam did a lot of damage to Gawr, but not quite enough to finish him off. So the people of Fargone locked him in a ginormous underground dungeon, fortified with a binding enchantment to keep him weak, and banished the rest of the giants to the land beyond the mountains. No giant has been seen in Fargone since, and Gawr has remained imprisoned . . . until now.'

Everybody goes quiet for a second.

'So the Cariad has gone?' Teg finally whispers.

'A few weeks ago, according to this message,' says Branwen, tapping the scroll. 'It says Gawr sprang a surprise attack on Llew, and managed to defeat him.'

'B-but how?' I ask. 'You said Gawr was locked up in a dungeon!'

Branwen shrugs helplessly. 'I don't know. The key is kept safe here in the palace! I can't imagine how he managed to escape . . . and now he's got the Cariad.'

'And that's why all the magical animals are switching types,' says Teg.

'Types?' asks Branwen.

'Oh, I've got so much to tell you,' says Teg excitedly. 'You see, I've been working on this theory –'

I groan. 'Can we not do this now?'

Teg grins. 'Sorry, not the right time. But, in brief: all over Fargone, magical creatures are getting their powers mixed up. That's why Cantre'r Awyr has started drifting apart and falling: because the starswans have lost their power. Gawr must have used the Cariad to change the crafancs from water creatures into air creatures, and at the same time he's upset the balance of all the other magical creatures in the land!'

'That makes sense,' says Branwen.

'But there are still two things that *don't* make sense,' says Lippy.

'Just two?' asks Roo.

'Firstly, *how* did Gawr escape his prison, especially if it was enchanted?' she continues, thoughtfully. 'And secondly . . . *what* are he and the crafancs up to?'

A silence settles over us, into which Branwen sighs. She lays her head on the table with her forehead flat against the surface. Lippy shuffles over and puts a hand on her shoulder.

'Are you OK?' she asks.

Branwen sighs. 'It's much harder being queen than I thought, you know. The whole world has started falling apart, and I've been too busy sitting for royal portraits and babysitting spoilt princes to notice.'

And then Lippy is hugging her tightly, and Branwen's entire being softens. She lifts her head, an affectionate smile appearing on her face.

'In Wales, we call this a *cwtch*,' Lippy explains. 'They fix basically everything.'

'You told me there's no magic in Wales,' says Branwen, 'but this is the most magical thing I've ever experienced.'

Lippy raises her eyebrows at the rest of us, expectantly. 'Group *cwtch*?'

Teg, Roo and I rush forward until we're all wrapped in one big *cwtch*. Blodyn rests her head against Lippy's shoulder, sprinkling a light dusting of snow over us, and Cadno leaps up on to his hind legs, squeezing between me and Roo, his sparks under control for once.

When we break apart, Branwen looks grateful.

'It's not your fault you didn't know, Branwen,' I say. 'The messenger was delayed, remember?'

Branwen nods, although she still looks a bit sorry for herself. But then her head snaps up.

'The messenger,' she says suddenly.

'What about the messenger?' asks Lippy.

'They weren't delayed by *chance*, were they?' Branwen replies, eyes widening. 'They were shot by an archer! Somebody didn't want this information to reach me. You don't just *accidentally* shoot somebody with an arrow, do you?'

'Oh, I don't know,' says Roo sheepishly. 'I've accidentally shot Charlie a few times in the multi player mode of *Pirates vs Cowboys*.'

'I don't know what that means,' says Branwen, and then she brandishes the scroll like a sword. 'But I do know we need to talk to the messenger. To the infirmary!'

Chapter 11

I lose count of how many lefts, rights, lefts, rights and then lefts again we take before we get to the infirmary. Branwen pauses halfway down one corridor and points at a tapestry on the wall.

'Look,' she says.

We gather round, and there, on the wall before us, is a woven scene depicting a great creature standing on the peak of a mountain: a mighty beast with the face of a lion, a flowing golden mane catching the sunlight to create a glowing halo, and giant padded front paws poised proudly on the rock. A pair of eagle wings are spread wide into the air behind it, its hind legs ending in a pair of talons.

'*Llew*,' I breathe.

'Glorious, isn't he?' says Branwen, staring wistfully at the tapestry.

'I . . . I can't believe a creature as mighty as that could be defeated,' I say.

'I know.' Branwen sighs. 'Come on.'

When we get to the infirmary, we find a familiar – yet somewhat unwelcome – figure loitering outside. Prince Efnisien is pacing back and forth in the hallway, a frustrated look on his face.

'Hey, Effy,' says Branwen as we march towards him. 'What're you doing here?'

'I've told you to stop calling me that!' Prince Efnisien snaps, but then he straightens up, like he's just realized how sharp his tone was. 'I'm here to check on that poor messenger. As soon as I heard about him, I came hurrying down to see if he was OK.'

Branwen narrows her eyes. 'That's very . . . *nice* of you.'

'I *am* nice,' the prince retorts, not very nicely. 'Anyway, what are *you* doing here?'

Branwen crosses her arms. 'Same as you.'

Efnisien snorts. 'Well, good luck. Catrin chucked me out. Said no visitors; he needs rest. I wouldn't bother if I was you.'

'Yeah, but I'm the queen,' says Branwen, and opens the door to the infirmary. 'See you later, cuz.'

We follow, but not before I see the prince roll his eyes.

'Don't I know it,' I hear him mutter as he skulks away.

The infirmary is a long, wide room with beds on either side, but only one is occupied at the moment. We hurry over to it, where we find a woman dressed in a white dress and cap applying a damp cloth to the head of a man whose eyes keep fluttering open and closed like he's in the middle of a bad dream.

He doesn't look very well.

'Nurse Catrin,' says Branwen. Catrin stops her dabbing and looks up, a fraught expression on her face.

'Your Majesty,' she says, dipping her head.

'Is this the messenger?'

'It is, Your Majesty.'

'Could we have a word?'

'He really isn't very well, Your Majesty.'

'We'll only be a moment,' Branwen insists. 'I wouldn't ask if it wasn't important.'

The nurse hesitates, but then nods and leaves the room.

Branwen approaches the messenger. His forehead is glistening, and there's a thick wad of bandages wrapped round his left shoulder, where the arrow hit him.

'Hello,' she says softly. 'My name is Branwen. You're in good hands here. Catrin has been removing my splinters since I was a baby.'

'T-this is a bit more than a splinter, Your Majesty,' the man says weakly.

Branwen smiles. 'Arrows are just very big splinters, aren't they? You'll be right as rain in no time.'

The man smiles, clearly reassured by Branwen's kind tone.

'I was wondering,' she says, 'if you'd be able to tell me a bit more about what happened at Cariad's Keep.'

'A t-terrible battle between Gawr and Llew.' The man coughs. 'Gawr sprang an a-attack on the sunlion under cover of darkness and b-bested him. N-nobody has seen Llew since.'

We all exchange nervous glances.

'And Gawr?' I ask. 'Do you know what Gawr is doing?'

The man's eyes widen, fear dancing behind his pupils. 'He's used the Cariad to take to the skies, and enlisted those a-awful crafancs to build a fortress in the clouds. Just look to the north; you can't miss it.'

We all look instinctively out of the window but, of course, we don't see anything. I'm not sure it even faces north. But still, knowing that Gawr is up there somewhere, probably plotting something terrible, makes me shudder.

'But what does he want?' Branwen asks, leaning in closer.

'He wants to rule F-Fargone, Your Majesty – both land and sky.'

At that, the whole room goes still. You could hear a snabbit sniff, it's so tense.

Lippy steps forward to put a hand on the queen's shoulder. 'Branwen –'

Just then, the messenger starts moaning in agony, a hand flying up to the bandage on his shoulder. We all leap back in fright as Nurse Catrin hurries through the door, a bowl of something green and gooey in her hands.

'With all due respect, Your Majesty, that's quite enough,' she insists. 'I need to apply some balm to fight the fever. You ought to leave.'

Branwen nods, numbly, and we follow her out of the room.

Back in the corridor, we stare at each other, none of us knowing quite what to say. Branwen looks like she wants to throw up.

'You don't have to face this alone,' I offer. 'We're here with you. We'll stop Gawr, just you see. We'll find Llew and get the Cariad back. Right?'

'Right,' says Branwen, giving me an appreciative smile. 'Thanks, all of you. You make being queen so much easier.'

'But we have one very small problem,' says Roo.

'What's that?' I ask.

'We all told our parents we'd be home by teatime.'

With a sinking feeling, I realize he's right. With all the floods, our parents will be worried sick if we don't return home.

'What if we send your dads a letter?' Lippy suggests.

Branwen beams. 'That's a brilliant idea! Lippy, you're so clever.'

Lippy blushes furiously, which is still a weird sight, seeing as how she's the least shy person ever.

'The portal is still open, isn't it?' says Branwen. 'I'll send a messenger to deliver the letter. You can say you're safe and enjoying the nice weather here in Fargone for a few days. They won't even know anything bad is happening!'

'And we'll ask your dads to tell *our* parents we're

staying at yours for a little while,' Lippy adds. 'They'll understand. We've been cooped up in our houses for ages; it's only natural that we've all missed each other.'

'Perfect,' I say.

'That does sound like a foolproof suggestion,' says Roo, who looks like he's trying very hard to find a way for it not to be.

'It's decided, then,' says Branwen, hands on her hips and looking very much like a queen once more. 'We're going to save Fargone.'

'Again,' Roo mutters.

Branwen grins. 'Again.'

Chapter 12

The plan is this: we're going to travel to the mountain grotto where the Cariad was kept, and where the battle between Llew and Gawr took place. When we get there, we're going to look for clues to the sunlion's whereabouts, in the hope that we can find him and enlist his help to defeat the dastardly giant.

But, like, properly this time.

'Gawr seems to be using the Cariad to sow magical chaos across the land,' says Teg, back in the Map

Room. 'So if we get it back, we can hopefully restore balance.'

'You mean, all the magical creatures will switch back to their usual types?' I say, my eyes lighting up.

'I think so.'

'You hear that, Cadno?' I exclaim. 'You'll turn back into a firefox!'

Cadno yips happily, and Blodyn stomps her hoofs in a hopeful display.

'The only problem is getting there,' says Branwen, leaning over the map table. She points at a mountain range. 'The path to Cariad's Keep up in the Carreg Mountains is perilous. We're looking at a two-day journey on horseback, but we don't have two days to spare.'

We all sit down, scratching our heads and coming up with nothing. Feeling stumped, I push away from the table and growl in frustration.

'Urgh! There *must* be a way to get there faster!' I huff. 'This is Fargone! There's magic everywhere!'

'Yes, but it isn't behaving like it's supposed to,

remember?' says Teg.

'How about flying?' I say. 'Have aeroplanes been invented here yet?'

'Eh?' Branwen gapes.

'I'll take that as a no.'

'Short of getting the wotters to carry us, there's no way we can fly,' says Teg. 'It's not like we've got a hot-air balloon, is it?'

'That's it!' cries Lippy, making us all jump. 'Branwen, you mentioned that you've been sitting for tons of portraits and tapestries, right?'

'Why are you reminding me?' Branwen groans.

Lippy rolls her eyes. 'Let me finish. What if we stitch some of them together to create a giant balloon? We might not have Cadno's fire any more, but we do have the seahorses, and they could use their fire bubbles to keep it in the sky!'

'And Kevin's air blast can pump the bubbles up!' Teg beams. 'Oh, the little dude is going to be absolutely chuffed to be doing something so heroic.'

I gawp at him, and Teg blinks.

'What?'

'You just said *dude*.'

'Yes, well, I've heard you call Cadno that lots of times. Did I use it properly?'

'You did, actually,' I tell him, and Teg grins proudly.

'This is bonkers,' says Roo.

'Completely,' I add.

'Yes,' Branwen agrees. 'But the best ideas usually are, aren't they?'

Roo blinks. 'Er. Come again?'

'Lippy, you're a genius! I could kiss you!' Branwen declares, and then she stops short. Roo and I share a smirk while Lippy and Branwen look anywhere but at each other, the queen suddenly fussing with a chip on the map's edge.

'Ahem,' she goes on. 'As I was saying, Lippy's idea sounds like our best shot. And as Queen of Fargone, I have a team of seamstresses and tailors at my beck and call. They can get to work on sewing those tapestries and paintings together. In the meantime, you can write a letter to Charlie's dads. Are we in agreement?'

'I think it's a rotten idea,' comes a voice from near the floor.

We look down, and there's Albanact, who's been so quiet throughout our visit that I'd actually forgotten he was with us. His arms are crossed and he's frowning like he's just stood on a piece of Lego.

'And why's that, Albie?' asks Teg.

'It just is,' Albanact replies. 'I've heard *awful* things about the Carreg Mountains. Lots of . . . er, loose boulders.'

'Loose boulders?' Teg repeats.

'Yes.'

'*Ooooo-kay*,' says Branwen, clapping her hands. 'Can anybody think of any *good* reason why we shouldn't proceed?'

We all shake our heads.

'So, just to be clear,' says Roo, 'we're going to fly across a strange country in a hot-air balloon made from tapestries, powered by the fiery bubbles of a bunch of flying seahorses and a fluffy hairdryer?'

'Yes,' says Lippy, like this is the most obvious thing ever.

'Great.'

Branwen grins. 'All right. We've got our plan, so now let's get to work.'

We spend the next hour writing a letter to my dads, trying to find the exact words that will convince them that nothing untoward is happening and that this is just an innocent extended holiday to Fargone. Eventually, we settle for something simple:

Dear dads,

Just a quickie to tell you that we're having lots of fun in Fargone. The weather is proper nice here, and Branwen has a new slide that we're having the best time playing on. We really don't want to come back to the rain just yet, and school is closed, so we thought we would stay for another couple of days. Could you please tell Lippy's and Roo's parents that they're having a long sleepover at our house

because we've missed each other so much?
  Wish you were here!
  Love,
  Your Charlie x

I don't think they'll be happy that we've gone against their instructions, but heigh-ho. At least they won't think we're up to anything dangerous.

Branwen takes the letter from us and summons a raven in a gleaming silver breastplate and tiny helmet, whispering something into its ear before it flies out of the window clutching the note.

'Express delivery,' she says, with a smile. 'Never fails, no matter the weather. Your dads will have their letter today.'

Meanwhile, what appears to be an entire army of seamstresses and tailors have arrived at the palace, armed with baskets full of fabric, needles, pins, scissors and glue. They disappear into a huge room called the Gallery and get to work.

Within an hour, they have stitched together dozens

of tapestries, forming a giant circle that takes up half the floor, growing with every passing minute.

'Awh, look at this one!' Lippy squeals, running over to a portrait of Branwen the size of a slice of toast.

'Yes, all right,' Branwen mutters.

'You look so small and cute!' Lippy coos, squidging Branwen's cheeks between forefinger and thumb. Branwen grumbles, but I can see it's pretend. 'And look, you're even smiling!'

'Because it was so tiny it took, like, ten minutes,' says Branwen, and then she pauses. 'Hey, why don't you keep it?'

Lippy's face lights up. 'Seriously?'

'Yes, of course. Too small to be of any use in the balloon.' She plucks it from the wall and hands it to Lippy. 'But the *perfect* size to fit in a pocket, don't you think?'

Lippy grins. 'Next time we come to Fargone, I am so bringing my phone. We can have our first selfie together!'

Branwen blinks. 'A . . . a *selfie*, you say?'

'It's a photograph you take of yourself.'

'A *photograph*? I don't understand.'

Lippy rolls her eyes. 'I'll show you one day.'

Then she and Branwen set off across the room to survey the progress of the seamstresses, hands linked like a pair of happy wotters.

'Ugh, they're so cute,' says Roo.

'Yep,' I agree. 'When do you think one of them is going to ask the question?'

Roo's eyes widen. 'No . . . Do you really think . . . ?'

I nod. 'Come on, Roo. You're not *twp*, are you?'

'OK, fine, you're right,' he replies, and then he puffs up his cheeks and blows all the air out. 'This is massive, though. None of us has had a boyfriend or girlfriend before.'

Chapter 13

At last, after hours of cutting and trimming, stitching and sewing, our hot-air balloon – which we decide to name the Fargone Falcon – is ready.

I must admit, even with the number of people who have been working on it, I'm impressed by how quickly they managed to pull it off. It's carried out into the courtyard, where a crowd of people awaits us, showering us in flower petals and offerings of food for the journey.

Finally, it's time to inflate the balloon for the first

time. In place of a basket that hangs underneath, we use one of the Gallivant Menagerie's carriages. This one has a sunroof, so we can easily climb in and out through the ceiling. Teg summons Albanact and the fiery flying seahorses, and we watch as they ready themselves before the lip of the balloon, which is currently still draped flat across the palace courtyard.

A couple of men hold the mouth of the balloon open, and the next stage begins.

'Cold air first,' Teg commands. I'm not sure if he's flown a balloon before, but he sounds like he knows his stuff.

Blodyn and Kevin step forward. Blodyn, pleased to finally have a good use for her new power, sends puffs of snowy air towards the mouth, which Kevin then pushes inside using his air blast. The balloon slowly starts to inflate.

After a while, Teg orders the cold air to be swapped for hot. Blodyn steps away and the flying seahorses charge forward.

'Do your thing, guys,' says Teg.

The seahorses get to work, producing flaming bubbles that, with a little help from Kevin's air blast, disappear inside the mouth of the balloon. As the air inside warms, it really starts to take shape, lifting into a sphere that seems to fill the entire sky above the courtyard.

The crowd lets out a chorus of *oohs* and *aahs*.

'Oh, wow,' I say. 'It's . . . er . . .'

'It's *something*,' Roo puts in.

'It's brilliant!' Lippy exclaims.

Truth be told, it's a bit scary. The top is almost completely formed of an enormous close-up of Branwen's face. The balloon is so full of air it's made her eyes look freakishly big, almost like she's staring out over all of Fargone. Her face is everywhere – huge ones, bigger than the surface of a trampoline, medium ones the size of a hula hoop and smaller ones that fill in the gaps, all of them stitched together to create the enormous floating mosaic that we see before us.

'Ha!' Branwen toots. 'Now I really think you can see the *essence of my spirit*!'

She turns to face the crowd, wearing a valiant expression befitting a queen.

'People of Fargone,' she declares, 'we are once again under threat. The Cariad has been stolen by none other than Gawr himself, who has somehow managed to escape his dungeon and spring an attack upon Llew, the mighty sunlion. Gawr has used the Cariad to change the crafancs into air creatures to help him build his fortress in the sky, and now other magical creatures are getting their powers mixed up, and Cantre'r Awyr is beginning to fall.'

The crowd murmurs with worry, but Branwen holds her hands up, silencing them.

'But fear not,' she goes on, 'for Charlie the Legendary and his friends have returned to rescue us from peril!'

At this, hope fills their faces. They begin to whisper among themselves, pointing at us and standing on tiptoes to get a good look. My cheeks flush.

'Under my leadership, we will travel together to find Llew,' Branwen announces. 'And then we will take our company to Gawr and chuck him out of his sky fort for good!'

The crowd starts cheering. Branwen really is a natural at this. She plays the part of queen very well. Her face is set with sparkling determination.

'Once we've done that, we will reclaim the Cariad and return Fargone to its former glory!'

By now, the crowd is ecstatic. They're jumping and applauding and punching the air. But then something shifts. I spot Prince Efnisien at the front of the crowd – and he's *laughing*. He points at Branwen, and then other people start joining in, their cries of excitement switching to laughter until the whole crowd is roaring.

'Are they laughing at me?' Branwen mutters out of the corner of her mouth, while she keeps trying to smile. 'Is he getting them to laugh at me?'

'No-no, of course not,' Lippy stammers in confusion. 'They're laughing *with* you, not *at* you – Oh, Branwen, you . . . erm . . . you have a moustache.'

'What?!'

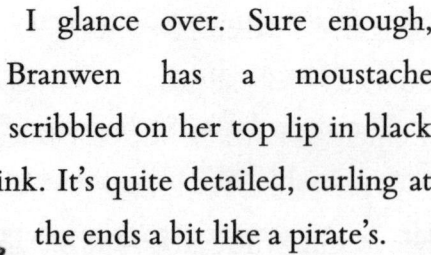

I glance over. Sure enough, Branwen has a moustache scribbled on her top lip in black ink. It's quite detailed, curling at the ends a bit like a pirate's.

'Don't be ridiculous,' says Branwen, bringing her hand up to her lips. Her fingers come away smudged, and she lets out a horrified gasp. 'Oh my gosh, I've got a moustache. *How have I got a moustache?*'

'I don't know,' I squeak. 'It wasn't there a second ago!'

Branwen scrubs furiously at her skin with her sleeve. 'How can a moustache just *appear* on me? Oh, look,' she wails, gesturing at the crowd, which is still busy guffawing. 'I've lost them! I'm nothing but a court jester to them now!'

'You haven't lost them,' Lippy hisses. 'Look, come here. I'll sort you out.'

And then, using the method handed down to us by grandmothers all over the country, Lippy pounces, using her newly licked thumb to scour Branwen's lip. Branwen kicks and flails, but Lippy is relentless, and a moment later the moustache is barely a shadow.

'I bet Effy is behind this,' Branwen growls, eyeing her cousin, who still hovers on the edge of the crowd, looking very self-satisfied.

'I don't think he can be,' I say apologetically. 'The moustache just sort of . . . appeared. He was nowhere near you.'

The queen huffs in resentment.

'There you go, you're all done,' says Lippy. 'Take a nice deep breath and carry on. You've got this.'

Branwen spares her a grateful smile and clears her throat. The crowd finally starts to settle again.

'Apologies for that little . . . er . . . *performance*,' says Branwen, reassuming her hands-on-hips pose. 'Now, where was I . . . ? Oh yes! We will reclaim the Cariad and return Fargone to its former glory once and for all! It is time to restore peace and balance to this beautiful queendom we call home!'

And, just like that, the crowd is lapping it up again.

Branwen turns and gestures for us all to enter the carriage. Above it, the hot-air balloon looms so large it's blocking out the light of the sun.

'All aboard!' she declares. 'Teg, I appoint you captain of the Fargone Falcon's maiden voyage!'

Teg beams. 'I won't let you down, Your Majesty!'

'They'll make anybody captain these days,' Albanact scoffs. 'Another reason why this is a bad idea and we should think of another plan that involves going *nowhere near those mountains.*'

Roo shuffles up the ladder and peers inside. 'There aren't any seatbelts.'

'Roo, get in,' Branwen mutters. 'You're holding up the queue. You too, Albanact.'

Roo lets out a reluctant sigh and enters, followed by Branwen, Teg and Kevin, Lippy, Blodyn, Cadno, a furiously complaining Albanact and, finally, me. I turn and give the crowd a last wave before the door closes.

'Thank goodness for that,' says Branwen, with a relieved sigh. 'What was that all about? How did a moustache suddenly appear on my face?'

'Beats me,' I say, 'but try to forget about it. You had them all in the palm of your hand.'

Branwen's face lights up. 'Do you think so? I try so hard to be a good queen.'

'You're an *amazing* queen,' Lippy assures her, but before she can say anything else, the carriage trembles underfoot. Roo lets out a terrified squeak, and Cadno ripples all over with nervous electricity.

'Buckle up,' says Teg, climbing up a rope ladder through the hatch in the roof. 'It's time for take-off.'

'Buckle up with what?' Roo exclaims, panicked.

'Just brace yourselves,' Teg snaps, his head reappearing through the hatch. 'The wind is on our side, so the Fargone Falcon can finally take flight!'

With that, the carriage lifts slowly into the air, and we all watch at the window as the courtyard shrinks beneath us, the faces of the crowd getting smaller and smaller.

'We're flying!' I cry. 'We're really flying!'

'Well, of course we're flying,' says Teg, peering

down from his place on the roof. 'Did you really doubt the seahorses? They're doing a stellar job, you know.'

As though in response, we hear a triumphant *toot* from above.

Lippy twirls round to face us, wearing an excited expression. 'Welcome aboard this Gallivant Airways flight from Talarwen to Cariad's Keep. In the event of an emergency, the exits can be located here –' she points at the closed door – 'and here.' She points at the roof hatch. 'Although we are expecting a smooth flight, if we do experience any turbulence, I would like to advise you to put your head between your knees and kiss your butt goodbye –'

'Lippy, stop!' Roo moans.

'Have a safe and enjoyable flight,' Lippy finishes, with a grin.

We're really high now, the palace shrunk to nothing but a series of squares and rooftops. Around it is the sprawl of Talarwen, Fargone's capital city, streets spiralling like a spiderweb, and around *that* are the jigsaw fields of the countryside, lines of trees knitting them together like a big emerald blanket.

It's a dazzling sight, even if Roo's cheeks have turned a bit green.

After a while, ghostly white wisps start to float past the window.

'Clouds!' Branwen exclaims, pointing.

She's right. We're climbing into a world of white now, every window looking out into cloud, so that for a few moments it appears as though we're buried under an avalanche. But then the clouds drop away and we're rising above them. I grin at the sight of the fluffy white carpet stretching to the horizon in every direction.

Finally, we stop climbing, and a peace unlike anything I've ever experienced settles over us.

'It's . . . it's beautiful,' Lippy whispers.

I have to agree. Up here, there is no noise, no traffic, no nothing. Just endless blue above and endless white below.

'Well, now we've reached maximum altitude,

there's nothing much to do except chill,' says Teg through the ceiling hatch. I peer upward and spot the flying seahorses, happily burping fiery bubbles into the mouth of the balloon.

Lippy, Branwen and Blodyn sit together in one corner, laughing and giggling. I play games with Cadno, swiping my hands at his face so that he opens his mouth and gently tries to catch them in his jaws.

After a while, Roo lets out a sigh from across the carriage.

I look up and see a sad expression on his face.

'Hey,' I call over to him. 'What's up?'

Roo shakes his head. 'Oh, nothing.'

'Roo, I'm your best friend. I know when something's up. Come on, scoot over here and talk to Charlie and Cadno.'

Roo reluctantly shifts over so that he's sitting next to me. Cadno nudges at his fingers with his nose – thankfully spark-free – and Roo gives a feeble smile.

'What's wrong? Are you still feeling travel-sick?'

'No,' says Roo, and then he hesitates. 'It's just that . . . well . . .'

'Come on, you don't have to be worried about sounding stupid around me.'

'Fine. It's just, you and Cadno have got your thing, and Lippy, Branwen and Blodyn have got their thing, and I'm just sort of like a gooseberry in the middle.'

'Roo, you are not a gooseberry!' I insist.

'Feels like it,' he mutters, and then he nudges his head towards Lippy and Branwen. They're roasting marshmallows on one of the seahorses' fire bubbles, and a chuckling Branwen is reaching out to swipe a bit of melted marshmallow from the tip of Lippy's nose. 'I mean, would you look at those two? They're not even officially going out yet and they're already winning Fargone's Cutest Couple Award.'

He's got a point. Lippy and Branwen *are* becoming unbearably adorable with every passing hour they spend in each other's company.

'Where has this come from?'

Roo sighs. 'I dunno. I come from a big family. It's hard to stand out. And now I'm part of the Adventure Squad, it feels even harder to stand out.'

'But you do! You're Roo the . . . the . . .'

'See? I'm just Roo, friend of Charlie the Legendary and Lippy the Radiant. Most people just glance over me. I just . . . I want something that's mine. I want what you've got with Cadno, or what Lippy's got with Blodyn.'

My heart goes out to him. Sure, Roo is close with both Cadno and Blodyn, but there's no doubting where their first loyalties lie. Even now, Cadno is giving Roo's fingers a good lick while his bum remains firmly planted on my lap.

'I just wish sometimes that I had my own magical friend to bond with, or that I could do something heroic,' he goes on.

'You've done lots of heroic things!'

'Like what?'

'Like . . . like . . .' I stammer, 'like when you fetched Edie's frisbee from up that tree the other week. That was *proper* heroic.'

Roo glares at me, deadpan. 'Really? The frisbee incident?'

'I couldn't think of anything on the spot, OK?'

Roo sighs again. 'It's all right. I know I'm useless.'

'You are *not* useless, Roo. You are brave and funny and the best sort of friend anybody could ask for.'

Cadno lets out a yip of agreement. Roo smiles half-heartedly, running his hands over the ex-firefox's fur. Cadno closes his eyes in contentment and leans into Roo's touch.

'Everybody, look to the right!' Teg shouts from above. 'We have company!'

Roo and I hurry to the window, where Lippy, Branwen and Blodyn are already gawping.

Gliding along next to us is a squadron of what I can only describe as giant manta rays. They have smooth grey skin and enormous wings like beautiful diamonds, which soar elegantly through the sky.

'Aerorays!' Teg calls down. 'They usually have command over electricity, a bit like Cadno does now. It would seem we're sailing Fargone's famous Sky Seas.'

'Sky Seas?' I echo, and then gasp as more creatures come into sight: a streamlined seal that spirals and corkscrews round the carriage; an airborne forest of dreamy pink jellyfish that bob slowly upward, trailing

their frilly tentacles behind them; a hammerhead shark emerging from a reef of clouds.

'Watch out below!' Teg cries, just as something enormous breaks the surface of the clouds beneath us.

It's a humpback whale, I realize, its stocky body soaring into the air only thirty metres or so from the carriage. It slows as it reaches its peak, twirls elegantly, and then slides back under the clouds on its hump, like an actual whale breaching the surface of the sea.

'Wow,' I breathe. 'That was *magnificent*.'

'Can't get too close,' Teg calls from above. 'If they're anything like the ground creatures, these animals have probably got their powers all confused, too. Don't want to risk getting near a creature that isn't in control of its new magic.'

As though in response, one of the aerorays lets out a spurt, not of electricity, but of what appears to be a *spiderweb*, from between the two antennae-like fins on either side of its mouth. The net comes to hang between two clouds, the gossamer soft and fluffy in a way that makes me think the webs themselves are made from cloud. A flying dolphin has to swerve to avoid entanglement.

'Yikes.' Branwen grimaces. 'Everything is really messed up, isn't it?'

I nod as we slowly leave the Sky Seas behind, the airscape around us returning to a more desert-like lifelessness.

Until, that is, a dark shape appears in the distance.

Or, more accurately, a cluster of dark shapes.

They're largely formless at first, just black blobs on the horizon, even higher up than we are. But as we get closer, they begin to sharpen into buildings. There are whole islands of houses floating up in the sky, and there, above them all, is a colossal structure that looks like it's still being built.

Teg swings down from the roof and shuts the hatch in a hurry.

'Teg, what is that place?'

His expression darkens. 'That,' he says, 'is Cantre'r Awyr. Or what's left of it . . . And above that is Gawr's fortress.'

Chapter 14

I can't believe what I'm seeing. Even from this distance, Gawr's fortress is bigger than the rest of Cantre'r Awyr put together, soaring higher than the highest mountain, a wooden monstrosity in the sky. It seems unnatural that something like that could ever stay airborne, but Teg explains that Gawr must be using the power of the Cariad to keep it aloft.

'What are *those*?' asks Roo, pointing. The outside teems with little black dots, some of them fluttering up through the clouds, others drifting down.

'Those are the crafancs, busy building Gawr's fort for him,' says Teg, with a shudder. 'Horrid things, they are.'

I narrow my eyes and can just about make out the creatures that swarm all over Gawr's fortress. They're about as big as crocodiles, and covered in thick, bristly brown fur. They've got flat, flipper-like tails and a ridge of purple and red plates pointing up from the fur along their spines, a bit like a stegosaurus, except these look poisonous.

And then one of them turns, and I have to swallow a gulp.

The crafancs have huge sabretooth tusks protruding from their mouths, and, between them, rows of serrated teeth that look perfect for sawing and cutting and grinding. Lots of them have rocks clamped between their jaws, or beams of wood, which they are carrying up to the fortress from the ground.

'Phwoar! Ugly, aren't they?' says Roo, and then I notice something else.

'Look,' I say, pointing at the ground.

The crafancs are flocking to a spot in a field way below, where there seems to be a mountain of debris piled up, a pyramid of shattered wood and stone. The crafancs drift down to the pile, grab a piece of detritus each, and then carry it back up to the fortress like worker ants.

But that's not all. Trampling all over the surrounding fields are *dozens* of giants, tearing up trees and stomping on abandoned farm buildings, ripping off roofs and tossing them on to the pile for the crafancs to collect. They're all enormous, with hunched shoulders, straggly hair and bulging eyes, snapping tree trunks between their fingers like they're nothing more than twigs.

'It's not just Gawr,' Branwen whispers, horrified. 'This is a giant invasion!'

'Do you guys hear that?' says Lippy.

I do. It's quiet at first, but then louder, flying towards us across the clouds from inside Gawr's fortress.

It's a song. Or, rather, a chant, accompanied by the beat of drums so heavy I fear they might start an earthquake. The voice is gruff and booming, and I've no doubt that it belongs to Gawr himself. Worst of all, however, are the words, which send a chill down my spine that not even Blodyn's new ice powers could rival.

> *Crush her bones and grind her spine,*
> *Once she's gone, the crown is mine.*
> *But first I'll build my floating fort,*
> *To lay a siege upon her court.*

> *Ground below and sky above,*
> *Everything is mine – sort of.*
> *Soon Fargone will be mine to conquer,*

And I'll squish the queen's head like a . . .
erm . . . a conker!

The chant comes to an end, and an ominous silence settles over us. Branwen's cheeks have flushed, and Lippy is biting her lip, like she wants to say something but isn't sure what.

'What is it with giants and chanting?' I ask, in an attempt to dispel the awkwardness. 'All that *fee-fi-fo-fum* nonsense.'

'Yeah, and it wasn't even very good, was it?' Roo adds, forcing a laugh. 'The first verse was OK, but it fell apart in the second.'

He and I chuckle together, but when it becomes clear that Branwen isn't going to join in, we trail off.

'Gawr really does want to take over the country,' Branwen whispers, staring into space. 'Once he finishes building his flying fort, he's going to attack.'

'Branwen . . .' Lippy says. 'There's no way he's going to . . . to crush –'

'How much longer until we reach our destination, captain?' snaps Branwen.

Teg glances out of the window. 'Actually, the Carreg Mountains should be coming into view any minute now.'

'Good,' says Branwen. 'You heard that stupid giant – he wants to crush my bones, and right now we're a bit too close for comfort. Oh, and there's the small matter of this balloon having my face *plastered all over it*! Might as well blow a horn to get his attention, eh?'

I can tell that, even though Branwen is trying to put on a brave face, she's shaken.

'Sure thing, Your Majesty,' says Teg, bringing a hand to his forehead in salute. 'Would you like to join me above as we begin our descent? Some fresh air might do you good.'

Branwen takes a deep breath. 'Yes. I would like that very much.'

It's chilly on top of the carriage. So chilly I wish Cadno still had his flames to keep us warm. The seahorses have eased off now, blowing their fiery bubbles at longer intervals, and gradually we begin to descend.

Mountains slowly begin to emerge through the clouds, snowy peaks with rocky grey slopes that turn to rolling green hills at their feet. The closer we get, the larger they loom, one of them jutting taller and craggier than the others.

'That's it,' says Branwen, eyes wide. 'That's Idris, the mountain where we'll find Cariad's Keep.'

We dip back through the clouds, the tension melting from Roo's body with every metre we sink. I peer over the edge of the carriage roof, bordered with a makeshift rope barrier.

We're low enough now that I'm able to make out details of the landscape once again: lumpy-bumpy hillocks covered in grass and interspersed with dense patches of gorse and the odd gnarled tree. There are villages scattered in the distance, too. The messenger in the infirmary must have come from one of them, I realize.

'Hmm, it's very uneven, isn't it?' says Teg, brow

furrowed. 'We'll need to find somewhere flat to land . . .'

'Oh yes, let's just keep going past these hills,' says Albanact hurriedly. 'No need to hang about *here*. If you keep going for a few miles, there's a riverbank that might be flatter.'

Teg narrows his eyes. 'How d'you know that, Albie? And why are you in such a rush to get over these hills?'

'I, er . . . I . . .'

'Come to think of it,' says Branwen, 'you've been acting strangely since we mapped our route back at the palace.'

Albanact looks affronted. 'I have *not* been acting strangely!'

'Hey,' Roo speaks up. 'What's that noise?'

We fall silent. At first I suspect maybe Gawr has started his ghastly chanting again, but instead, above the low whistle of the wind, there is another sound. This one is more high-pitched, almost a squeal, and it's getting louder with every passing second.

We all look up, and there, whizzing down through the clouds, is a little black dot. It's ricocheting this way and that, like a pinball, moving too quickly for me to be able to make out what it is. I can tell one thing, though . . .

'Erm, it's coming straight towards us,' I say, with an edge of alarm.

The shape gets bigger, and I catch a quick flash of brown fur and purple. Wait, are those *spines*? It's flying out of control, like a party balloon when you let all the air out. The sound isn't that different, either: a piercing squeak that rattles between my ears.

'Oh dear,' says Teg. 'This isn't good.'

'What do we do?' Roo shrieks.

'Remember what I said earlier,' says Lippy, slowly backing towards the roof hatch, 'about putting your head between your knees and kissing your butt goodb—'

'Not helping! Not helping!'

Suddenly we're all rushing for the hatch and dropping into the carriage, as though being inside a tiny wooden box will be any safer if we end up crashing. I'm the last one left up top, so I quickly pass Cadno to Lippy, who lets out a squeal as her hair stands on end, Cadno's body rippling all over with flustered sparks, and then I'm clambering inside.

My feet meet the floorboards, and the last thing I see before chaos unfurls is the fluffy, spiked creature colliding into the hot-air balloon above us with the most dreadful sound of all: a single echoing *POP!*

I glance at my friends, our faces fraught with terror, and then the balloon and its carriage both fall from the sky with us inside.

Chapter 15

We cling to one another, our screams drowning each other's out. This is it. We're goners. I close my eyes and think of my family, how I'll never see any of them ever again.

There's a *bang* and the carriage judders violently, cracks appearing in the walls as the wood splits, and suddenly the whole world starts spinning, as if we're caught in the belly of a giant washing machine. The roof becomes the floor, becomes the wall, becomes the roof again. My body collides

with somebody else's, knocking the air from my lungs . . .

. . . and then we are still.

Slowly, I open my eyes, a dull ache blossoming between my temples.

We're still inside the carriage – or what's left of it. I'm sprawled on what appears to be the roof, with the floor above us cracked open. I can just about see the crooked tips of branches curling over the fissure, like the fingernails of a giant witch trying to prise the carriage open. My friends are scattered about me in a knot of arms, legs and bumped heads, eyes blinking open and groans yawning from mouths.

But we're all, miraculously, still alive.

'Maybe next time I'll install an eject button,' comes Teg's voice from the jumbled pile of limbs.

'And some parachutes,' I manage to croak as I sit up.

I hear a yip, and Cadno bounds towards me, licking my face with such force that he almost knocks me over again. He's still sparking a little bit, but it doesn't matter. I hold him close, static rippling up my arms and tingling down to my fingertips.

Electrafoxes don't give the most comfortable *cwtches*, but in that moment I don't care.

'Are we all OK?' asks Branwen, crawling from the mass of bodies and rubbing a bump on her head.

'Yeah, I think so,' Lippy replies, peering out from around Blodyn. Even after a crash-landing, the frostdoe still manages to look elegant, a flurry of calming snow settling down on us as we attempt to gather our composure.

'My shell!' comes an anguished shriek from the corner of the ruined carriage.

I spot Albanact emerging from beneath a landslide of woven baskets. His face is twisted in distress, and for a moment I'm not sure what's going on, but then I realize what he's holding.

A fragment of shell.

Albanact turns and, sure enough, his snail shell has completely fractured. A spiderweb of cracks swirls out from the middle, and there's a hole at the top where a chunk has completely broken free – the chunk which is now clamped in his paws.

Before any of us can do anything, the snabbit throws his head back and lets out a grief-stricken wail.

'Albie, it's OK!' Teg assures him. 'Don't panic; we can fix it!'

'Oh, what am I going to do?' Albanact sobs. 'A snabbit is nothing without his shell!'

'Look, we can patch it all together again! A bit of tape, a spot of glue, and you'll be right as rain!'

'*Glue?*' Albanact howls. 'I'm not a model train!'

'Yes, yes, I know, Albie, but listen . . .'

Lippy, Branwen and I exchange pitying looks. And that's when I notice – I haven't heard a word from Roo since we crash-landed. Come to think of it, my friend is nowhere to be seen.

'Wait a minute, where's Roo?'

We all glance around, but there's no sign of him anywhere.

'Roo?' I call. '*Roo!*'

My heart starts to pound in a hummingbird panic all over again.

'I'm out here,' groans a familiar voice from outside.

Instantly, Lippy and I are heaving ourselves out through the hole in the floor and into the open. We've landed in a small copse of the gnarled trees that I spotted from the air, surrounded by gorse and those strange, pillowy hills. The carriage is caught upside down in the branches, like a fly in a spiderweb, which I guess explains how we're still alive. If we'd landed on the ground, we'd probably have been smashed to smithereens. The balloon is now completely flat, draped across the thorny bushes with the hooked barbs of branches jutting through the fabric.

And there, ensnared in a shredded patch of Branwen's giant woven nose, just a few feet from the ground, is Roo.

'Roo!' I exclaim, hurrying over. 'Oh, thank goodness you're OK!'

'I mean, I've felt better,' he grumbles, a stupefied

look on his face. 'Help me get down, will you? I feel like I'm in the world's worst hammock.'

Lippy and I get to work freeing him, but it's tricky. His legs are snared in twists of cloth, and he protests as we tug him loose.

'Careful! You're gonna rip my foot off!'

'Proper wedged in, aren't you?' Lippy grunts. 'How did you end up out here?'

'I dunno,' says Roo. 'I think the force of our landing chucked me out through the roof hatch at the very last second. Hey, what *was* that thing anyway – OUCH!'

'What?' I exclaim. 'What is it?'

'Something sharp jabbed me right in the butt – Aaaaaargh, there it is again! There's something in here with me! Get me out!'

Lippy and I grab his arms and heave. Roo finally slips free, sliding to the ground like a huge booger from Branwen's knitted nose. He scrambles away and glances back at the tapestry that had entangled him.

The three of us watch in horror as the fabric shifts, something moving underneath. I'm about to tell everybody to run, when a fluffy shape tumbles out and lands on the ground with a *plop!*

We stare, open-mouthed, at the mound of brown fur before us.

'W-what is it?' Roo stammers.

I open my mouth to answer, but then realize that I don't know. Whatever it is, it's small, barely bigger than a Labrador puppy. It's got purple and red spikes poking from its back and a flat, oval-shaped tail. And then it lifts its head, and we all scream.

'Argh!' Roo shouts. 'It's *hideous*!'

The creature has a pair of beady eyes, a black snout with long, wiry whiskers as thick as a rat's tail, and tiny, round ears right at the back of its head. Whatever it is, it's obviously an infant. But that doesn't make it any less unnerving to look at, because the main fear factor comes from its mouth.

From beneath its upper lip jut a pair of horrifying tusks. They look big enough to chomp through blocks of wood – or, at least, they would if one of them wasn't bigger than the other. The left one is smaller and blunter, so that its lip snaggles in a way that looks almost –

'*Adorable!*' Lippy squeals. 'Roo, don't be so cruel!'

I have to admit, Lippy is right. I had a fright at first, but now that the creature is ogling up at us, it really is quite sweet. It tilts its head and makes a sniffly, slobbery noise, almost like a piglet's *oink*.

'Adorable?' Roo hisses. 'It looks like something from my nightmares!'

'Step away from the crafanc!' comes a voice from behind us.

We whirl round, and there stands Teg on the floor-turned-roof of the upside-down carriage. Kevin, coiled round his shoulder, lets out a warning blast from his hairdryer nose. Branwen emerges from the wreck behind him, her eyes widening when she sees what's perched before us.

'The *what*? Did you say *crafanc*? As in, the monsters that Gawr has enlisted to help him build his fortress in the sky? The ones that *eat people*?!'

'That's an infant crafanc!' Teg confirms. 'All of you, back away . . . *slowly*.'

At my feet, Cadno's fur ripples with electricity. A low growl rumbles from his belly. Lippy, Roo and I start to retreat, slowly, not wanting to provoke the creature with any sudden movements . . .

But it's no use. The baby crafanc wriggles its bottom, front legs poised and ready to pounce – and then charges directly at us.

For the second time in ten minutes, I let out an ear-splitting scream. Cadno unleashes a bolt of lightning as the crafanc stampedes towards us, but he misses. The creature leaps through the air, a flash of pink tongue lolling hungrily from between its tusks, and soars straight at Roo.

It hits him in the middle of his chest, sending them both crashing to the ground, and Roo cries out in fear as the monster proceeds to . . . *nuzzle* him?

'Help, gerrimoffme!' Roo shrieks.

Next to me, Lippy's shoulders soften. 'Erm,

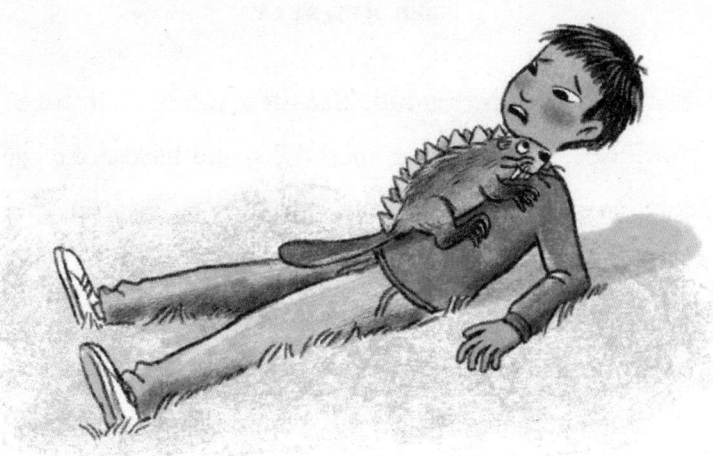

Roo . . . I think it likes you.'

'Wha–' Roo splutters, peering round the crafanc's fluffy, round body. It's sitting square on his torso, nuzzling its head against our friend's chin and squeaking happily.

'Fascinating,' says Teg, coming to stand next to us, along with Branwen. None of us makes a move to help Roo, even as he continues to whimper and squirm – but even those are becoming interspersed with the odd giggle, as though he's trying his very best not to laugh.

'What?' I ask.

'It would seem our balloon was popped by a rogue

crafanc,' Teg muses aloud. 'See those spines on its back? And those tusks? Either of those could have done the job, the prickly little menace. But what' *really* interesting is what it's doing down here in the first place.'

'As your queen, I command that you get to your point faster,' says Branwen.

'Well, crafancs are famously quite unpleasant,' says Teg. 'That's why they're usually referred to as water demons – or were before they became airborne, thanks to Gawr and his tricks. But look at this one . . . does it scream *man-eating beast* to you?'

We watch as Roo continues to writhe underneath the baby crafanc's affection. Its butt wiggles back and forth happily, its flipper tail batting up and down as it bombards our friend with slobbery kisses.

'Save me!' Roo cries.

'It's utterly horrifying,' Lippy drawls, a smile creeping on to her face. 'But why isn't it up there with the rest of the crafancs, helping to build Gawr's fortress?'

'My question exactly,' says Teg. 'Look at its tusks – one smaller than the other. And look at how friendly it is. My guess would be that this baby crafanc was the runt of the litter and was cast out by its parents for having one bad tusk, or for not being mean enough – or both. We just happened to be in the firing line when they chucked it out of the skies.'

Lippy's hand flies up to her mouth. 'That poor thing!'

'He can come with us!' I exclaim. 'Can't he, Teg?'

'Oh yes! We can look after him! Please, Teg?'

'Absolutely not!' Roo shouts from the ground. 'It's trying to savage me! Why is nobody helping, by the way?'

We ignore him. Teg puffs out his cheeks. 'I don't know; we've already got our hands full, haven't we? We've got Cadno, Blodyn, Kevin, Albanact –'

'But, Teg, you run the Gallivant Menagerie,' I urge. 'You can't turn away an animal in need!'

Teg glances over his shoulder, a pained look on his face. 'I know, but we're not at the menagerie any more. And the bit we brought with us isn't exactly doing very well, is it?'

'We can't just leave him,' says Branwen. 'He's already been abandoned by his own kind.'

Cadno wanders over to the baby crafanc and sniffs at its flipper tail. The creature whirls round and they meet, nose to nose. It lets out a playful *oink* and takes to the air, doing an ungainly somersault before crashing into Roo's belly all over again.

'Anyway, it looks like the final decision isn't up to me,' says Teg.

'What do you mean?' I ask.

'It's another theory I've been working on. In rare cases, I've observed unbreakable bonds forged between magical creatures and humans, almost like their souls are drawn together. Kevin has imprinted on me —' Kevin nestles in close to Teg's ear — 'and Cadno has imprinted on you, Charlie, and Blodyn on Lippy. And now, it would seem, this baby crafanc has already imprinted on Roo.'

Roo looks up, dumbfounded. '*Imprinted?*'

Lippy beams. 'Awwwwh, does the baby crafanc think Roo is its mummy?'

Roo snarls at her.

'Not exactly,' says Teg. 'More like a brother. There's no bond quite like that between a magical creature and its human. It is a friend, a sibling, a guardian, all wrapped up into one indestructible relationship.'

Roo finally manages to sit up. The baby crafanc settles down on his lap and stares up at him dotingly. It's the same way Cadno used to look at me when he was a young cub, and still does now.

'So you're telling me that you guys get a firefox and a floradoe,' says Roo, 'and I get . . . this thing.'

'Oh, Roo, don't be so cruel!' Lippy snaps. 'He needs you to look after him.'

Roo crosses his arms and looks away, but I can see him stealing the odd glance at his new companion. 'All right. Fine. He can stay. But he'd better keep those prickles to himself!'

The baby crafanc gives another happy *oink* and leaps up to bombard Roo with a fresh shower of kisses. Roo splutters, while Cadno and Blodyn both sniff curiously at their latest friend.

'That settles it, then,' says Teg. 'We have another addition to the party. Roo, you'd best think up a good name for him.'

At last, Roo clambers to his feet and brushes himself down. The crafanc flutters up to sit on his shoulder, except he really is a bit big for that, and Roo stumbles. The crafanc rolls down his front and lands in his arms so that Roo is cradling him like a baby. He stares lovingly up at him, while Roo looks a bit . . . well, *confused*.

'Where are we, anyway?' he asks, glancing around.

'We're in the hills leading up to the Carreg Mountains, where we'll find Cariad's Keep,' says Branwen. 'Perfect place to crash, really. Couldn't have got much closer if we'd tried.'

'Yes, yes,' comes a sniffy voice from behind us. We turn and see Albanact heaving himself out over the lip of the split carriage. He's holding his fragment of shell close to his chest. 'Come on, then. Let's make a move. No use hanging around here.'

The rest of us exchange perplexed looks.

'Erm, Albie, are you sure you're OK?' Teg asks. 'Maybe you should take it easy –'

'I am absolutely *fine*,' Albanact insists. 'I shall simply have to let go of my snabbithood and embrace my new identity as a . . . a plain old *rabbit*.'

'Well, well, well, what have we got here?'

It's a voice that I don't recognize, which makes me realize that it came from somebody we don't know. Somebody that isn't in our little party. Suddenly, I feel a hundred pairs of eyes on us, the hairs on the back of my neck standing on end.

We look up, and there, peering down at us, is a semicircle of faces. They've all got tall, hare-like ears and shiny, highly polished shells, and that's when it hits me.

'Oh dear,' Albanact mutters. 'Too late.'

We're surrounded by snabbits.

Chapter 16

I don't know why, but I'd never given any thought to the idea that there might be more than one snabbit. But of *course* there would be, just like when I learned that Cadno wasn't, in fact, the last of the firefoxes.

And right now there must be at least fifty snabbits, all of them gazing down at us from their vantage points on the hillocks surrounding the copse. One in particular stands out, its fur the fierce grey of a storm cloud, one hand propped on its hip and the other clasping a staff topped with feathers.

That must be the boss snabbit.

'Hello, Father,' Albanact grumbles miserably.

My head snaps round. Wait, did he just say –

'That's your *dad*?' Teg hisses.

The chief snabbit starts walking towards us, flanked by more snabbits carrying spears. Albanact's father is bigger than the others, his shell encrusted with all manner of gems.

'Nice of you to *drop* in,' the chief says, booming with laughter at his own joke. I didn't realize that something so small and unassuming as a snabbit could sound so commanding. 'You know, you could at least have written us a letter every once in a while. Your mother misses you terribly.'

'Sorry, Father,' says Albanact, not looking up.

The chief peers at Albanact's broken shell, a dismayed expression appearing on his face. 'And look what you've gone and done to yourself. You always were careless, even when you were but a bunny.'

'Sorry, Father,' Albanact mumbles again.

'Will somebody please explain what's going on?' I blurt.

The chief snabbit blinks at me. 'You look awfully familiar. Scruffy hair, funny red hat . . .' He pauses, his eyes widening. 'You're the one they call Charlie the Legendary!'

My cheeks flush. 'I, er . . .'

'It's a pleasure to make your acquaintance,' says the chief, reaching out to shake my hand. He may be the biggest snabbit, but his paw still feels small when enclosed in my grip. 'Everybody, bow down to Charlie the Legendary!'

'Oh, there really is no need –'

But it's too late. The other snabbits are all dipping into bows, a chorus of, 'All hail Charlie the Legendary!' fluttering over me like confetti.

'You and your friends are most welcome,' says the chief. 'But what are you doing with our Albie? Last time we saw him, he was running away to chase his dreams in the city. Always had ideas above his station, didn't you, Albie? Never really wanted to live the humble life of a snabbit. I did warn him that he was wasting his time, that snabbits aren't meant to bask in the limelight – didn't I, Albie?'

'It's *Albanact*, Father,' Albanact whines. 'And I'm the Deputy Camp Supervisor of the Gallivant Menagerie now!'

'And Royal Advisor to the Queen,' says Branwen, lips narrowed into a fierce smile.

'And *Royal Advisor to the Queen*?!' Albanact squeaks, his eyes nearly popping out of his head. Branwen arches her eyebrows at him in a way that says *just play along*, so Albanact returns his attention to his father, swallowing a gulp. 'Yes, and . . . er . . . Royal Advisor to the Queen.'

At that, the chief's gaze lands on Branwen. This time, it's *his* eyes that look like they're about to pop out of his head. He dips into another bow, the rest of the snabbits following suit.

'All hail Queen Branwen!'

'It is an honour to welcome you to our home,' says the chief, and then he nods his head at his son doubtfully. 'Tell me, what sort of advice would a queen like you be wanting from a snabbit like Albie?'

'I require Albanact's expertise on many topics,' Branwen says haughtily. 'Diplomatic relations, court proceedings and, erm . . . military tactics!'

'*Military tactics?*' the chief echoes in disbelief. 'Well, well, Albie . . . you certainly have done well for yourself, haven't you?'

'Y-yes,' Albanact says uncertainly, but then he puffs out his chest. 'Why, yes, I have, Father. I told you I would, didn't I?'

The chief throws up his arms. 'That's my boy! I never doubted you. Always knew you would go on to do great things.'

Albanact opens his mouth to object, but the chief hurriedly moves on.

'We watched your approach from home, and when we saw your aircraft fall from the sky, we hurried to your aid.'

'Wait a minute,' I interject. 'Did you say *home*?'

'Indeed,' says the chief. 'These hills are the ancient ancestral home of the snabbits. Has Albie not told you?'

'No,' I say, shooting a glare at Albanact. 'He hasn't.'

'Hmph,' says the chief, crossing his arms over his chest. 'Thought you'd just drift over in your fancy balloon without popping in to say hello, did you, Albie? Your mother will be very disappointed when she finds out.'

So this is why Albanact was so reluctant to embark upon this mission: because he knew it would take us close to his former home! And his *family* . . .

'Well, it would seem you're stuck here for now,' says the chief, pointing at the shattered carriage with the tip of his staff. 'So you might as well make yourselves comfortable with us. Don't worry, we'll have your aircraft up and running in no time. With a few improvements to it, I'll wager. That thing looks like it was built by a bunch of amateurs.'

Teg mutters something under his breath and kicks at the ground, suddenly embarrassed.

'Your shell, too, Albie. It looks like it was due an upgrade, anyway.'

The chief's shoulders sag when he sees our bemused expressions.

'Don't tell me,' he says. 'Albanact never mentioned his family's proud legacy? Our great talent for fixing and creating?'

We gawp blankly at him.

'*Talent?*' Roo whispers to me, the baby crafanc still lounging lazily in his arms. 'I thought he was just a snabbit.'

'Did you tell your friends *anything* about your heritage, Albie?'

Albanact looks away, and the chief lets out a grunt of frustration.

'Shame on you, Albie,' he growls. 'You should be proud of your snabbit blood! We might live our lives in these hills, away from the hustle and bustle, but that doesn't mean we don't have our uses. We may be small, but we're mighty in our own way. Now, come on, let's get you settled in.'

He turns and starts ambling towards the hills, the rest of the snabbits following him.

'I'm Chief Cadwaladr, by the way,' he booms over his shoulder. 'Welcome to the Warren!'

The Warren wasn't visible from the air – and that's because it's a network of tunnels built *into* the soft, lumpy hills. We enter through an unassuming hole in a nearby hillside, for a second enveloped by gloom and a damp, earthy smell. But then the passageway opens into a magnificent underground world.

These aren't the sort of tunnels you'd expect a rabbity creature to inhabit, full of dirt and bugs. Oh no. These tunnels are like an underground city. They're lit in warm yellow tones, with windows and doorways cut into the walls, ladders leading to upper levels and bridges spanning wide gaps.

And everywhere we look, there are snabbits. There must be hundreds of them, all different shapes and sizes, some of them pushing wheelbarrows piled high with brass cogs and glistening ore, others carrying

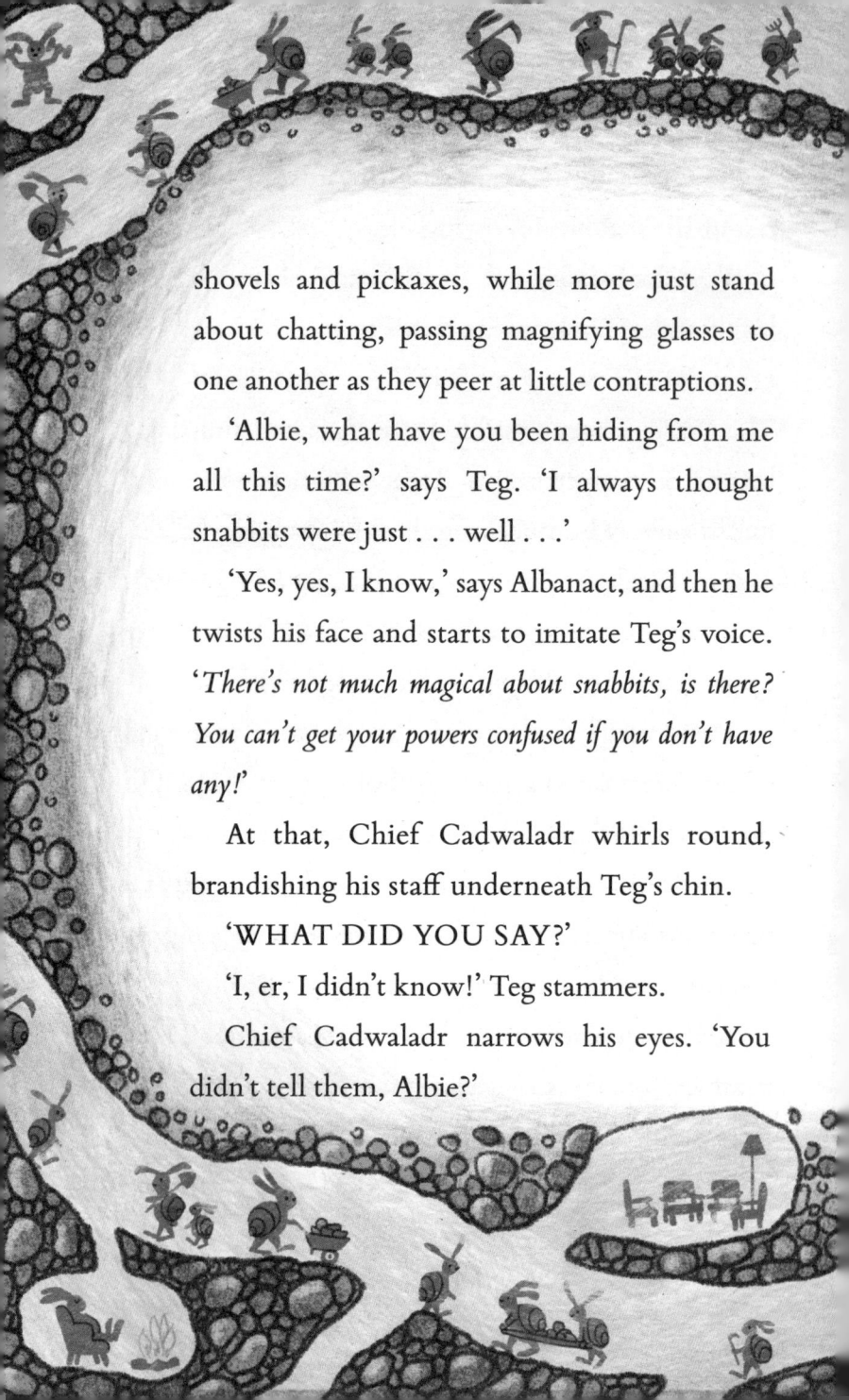

shovels and pickaxes, while more just stand about chatting, passing magnifying glasses to one another as they peer at little contraptions.

'Albie, what have you been hiding from me all this time?' says Teg. 'I always thought snabbits were just . . . well . . .'

'Yes, yes, I know,' says Albanact, and then he twists his face and starts to imitate Teg's voice. *'There's not much magical about snabbits, is there? You can't get your powers confused if you don't have any!'*

At that, Chief Cadwaladr whirls round, brandishing his staff underneath Teg's chin.

'WHAT DID YOU SAY?'

'I, er, I didn't know!' Teg stammers.

Chief Cadwaladr narrows his eyes. 'You didn't tell them, Albie?'

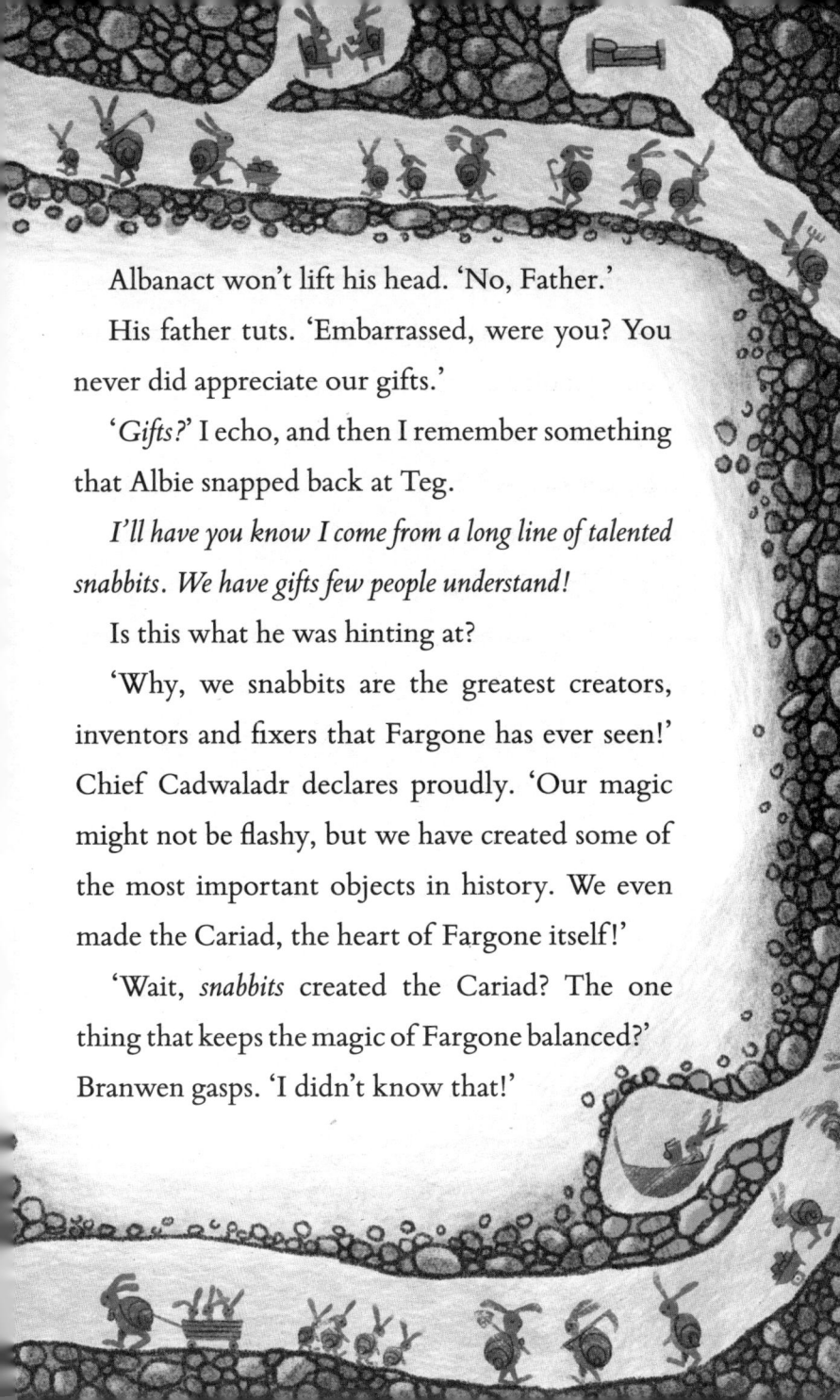

Albanact won't lift his head. 'No, Father.'

His father tuts. 'Embarrassed, were you? You never did appreciate our gifts.'

'*Gifts?*' I echo, and then I remember something that Albie snapped back at Teg.

I'll have you know I come from a long line of talented snabbits. We have gifts few people understand!

Is this what he was hinting at?

'Why, we snabbits are the greatest creators, inventors and fixers that Fargone has ever seen!' Chief Cadwaladr declares proudly. 'Our magic might not be flashy, but we have created some of the most important objects in history. We even made the Cariad, the heart of Fargone itself!'

'Wait, *snabbits* created the Cariad? The one thing that keeps the magic of Fargone balanced?' Branwen gasps. 'I didn't know that!'

Chief Cadwaladr smiles. 'Few do. We work in solitude here beneath the hills, rarely venturing out to the wider world.'

He shoots his son a glare. Albanact shrinks away. He's clearly one of the first snabbits ever to have wandered beyond the Warren.

'The Cariad was created by our ancestors, many thousands of years ago, to bring peace to the realm of Fargone,' Cadwaladr goes on, his smile dropping into a look of deep sadness. 'That was until it was stolen, of course.'

I remember then something that Teg said, too. It was only this morning, in the palace, but it feels like a lifetime ago. *An ancient artefact that was created to keep the magic of the land in balance, by a race of talented inventors, long since forgotten.*

He hadn't realized it, but he was talking about the snabbits!

'But that's why we're here!' I exclaim. 'We were on our way to Cariad's Keep to see if we could find any clues as to where Llew the sunlion has gone! We need his help if we're going to stand a chance of getting the Cariad back from Gawr.'

Chief Cadwaladr nods, knowingly. 'Yes, I daresay you will. Well, we can take you up to the keep.'

Branwen's face lights up. 'You can?'

'Indeed,' says the chief. 'But it's getting late. You all need rest and some patching up. Come on, Albie. Best not keep your mother waiting a minute longer.'

Chapter 17

Chief Cadwaladr's burrow is super cosy. There are towering bookshelves and a hearth with a roaring fire, a circle of armchairs before it. Albanact's mother, a big brown snabbit called the chieftess, almost drops the mixing bowl she's working over when she sees us walk in. She bustles over and wraps her son in a hug, then gives him a stern telling-off about staying away for so long.

'You could have written!' she snaps, in a voice that

makes me think that the chieftess is not to be crossed, despite her kind face and inviting burrow.

'Exactly what I told him,' says Chief Cadwaladr.

'I'm sorry, Mother,' says Albanact glumly. 'I got carried away with life on the road.'

The chieftess's expression softens. 'I forgive you. It makes me happy to know that you're achieving your dreams. *But don't do it again!*' She spots us standing there and her face lights up. 'Oh, and these must be your friends! Come in, let me show you around.'

We're shown around the burrow, from the kitchen to the study, eventually coming to a stop outside a closed door.

'This is our Albie's bunnyhood bedroom,' she says fondly. 'I haven't touched his prized pine-cone collection ever since he left for his travels. I've even left the googly eyes on them. Shall I show you inside?'

'No, Mother, let's not!' Albanact insists, shepherding her away, but the rest of us can't help giggling.

We're soon settled into the armchairs before the fire, with Blodyn and Cadno curled up on the floor and the baby crafanc climbing all over them. Blodyn huffs irritably, while Cadno closes his eyes, as good a smile as a fox can give working its way on to his mouth.

The chieftess carries over a tray laden with cups of warm milk, bowls of blackberries and a loaf of cinnamon-spiced apple bread with little tureens of salted butter, which might just be the most delicious thing I've ever tasted.

Meanwhile, Chief Cadwaladr waddles back in with a roll of parchment, which he spreads on the table before us. The paper looks old, so old I worry it might crumble to dust in front of us and ruin our supper.

'What's this?' I ask.

'We snabbits like to design our creations before we actually make them,' says the chief, pointing to the ink drawing in the middle of the sheet. It shows a heart-shaped shield, with what appears to be a jewel at its centre.

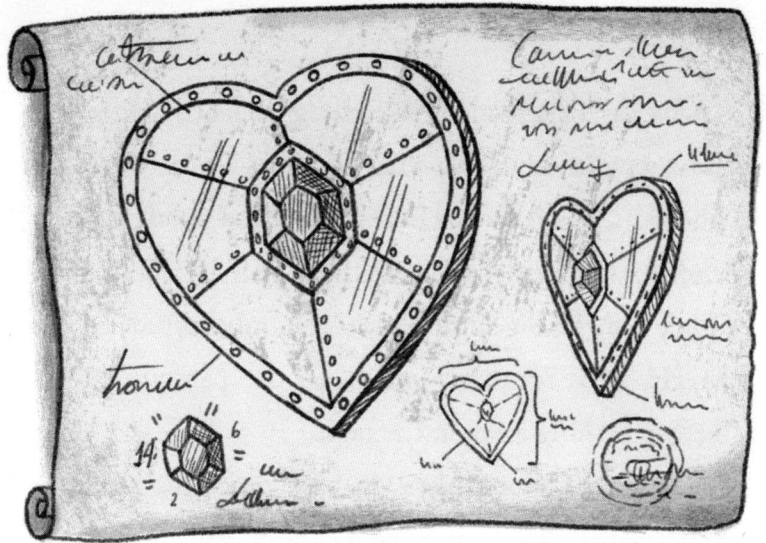

'This is the original design for the Cariad,' he explains. 'We keep every single sketch we make, even the very, very old ones.'

'*Wow*,' I say, absorbing the image and stamping it into my memory. 'So you're telling me that this shield is single-handedly responsible for protecting the magic of Fargone?'

'Told you snabbits aren't to be trifled with, didn't I?' says the chief, nodding proudly, but then his expression falls. 'But it's no good in the hands of Gawr, is it? He's used the Cariad to switch the powers of the crafancs for his own gain, and has brought chaos on Fargone by switching and confusing the powers of everything else. Of course, he's forgotten about us, nestled away in the hills. Everybody forgets about us snabbits, don't they? Especially the giants. They may be big, but they're certainly stupid.'

He sighs sombrely and rolls the parchment up, before coming to sit at the table.

'It seems to me like you have quite the story to tell,' says the chief, gesturing at all of us. We must be quite the sight. A firefox who's now an electrafox, a floradoe who's now a frostdoe, a baby crafanc, a snabbit with a shattered shell, a queen, and a group of children from another realm.

I launch into an account of our story so far, covering everything from the rain back in Wales, to all that's happened since our arrival in Fargone. The chief and chieftess listen, their faces slowly becoming graver the deeper I get into our tale.

'Oh dear,' says the chieftess, once I've finished. 'Oh dear, dear me.'

'You've been through an awful lot in a short space

of time,' says the chief. 'Well, fear not. We snabbits are nothing if not resourceful, so rest assured we can help you.'

I blink at them. 'Y-you can?'

The chief nods. 'We live our lives in the shadows of the Carreg Mountains. We often heard Llew's roar as he patrolled Cariad's Keep, and we watched helplessly when Gawr sprang his attack upon him.'

Branwen gasps. 'You *saw* the fight?'

'Indeed,' confirms the chief, his voice heavy. 'We snabbits are inventive and practical, but warriors we are not, so there was nothing we could do to help Llew as Gawr slung him from the sky. Attacked him from behind, Gawr did, just after sunset, when Llew was at his weakest. Otherwise, the mighty sunlion would surely have triumphed.'

'Did you see what happened to Llew then?' I press. 'What did Gawr do to him?'

The chief shakes his head. 'He carried him away, but we didn't see where.'

'I don't suppose you've noticed anybody suspicious passing through, have you?' asks Branwen, hopefully. 'Somebody who might have freed Gawr from his prison in the first place?'

Chief Cadwaladr shakes his head. 'I'm sorry, Your Majesty, but we've seen nobody.'

'It's OK.' Branwen sighs, then shakes her head, too. 'I just still don't understand how somebody got their hands on that key in the first place. The key is the only way to get round the enchantment. Open the door with the key, and the enchantment breaks, just like that. Gawr would have been able to regain his strength and attack Llew.'

'We have to go up to the keep,' I say determinedly. 'Look for clues.'

'Tomorrow, I will take you.'

'*Tomorrow?*' Branwen cries. 'But we don't have time to waste!'

The chief chuckles. 'Night has fallen, Your Majesty, and you will not find any clues in the dark.'

'And you could all do with a good night's

sleep,' says the chieftess, coming to stand next to Albanact, who's busy stuffing blackberries into his mouth. 'Oh, Albie. What are we going to do with you?'

'Don't worry, we'll fix him up,' says the chief. 'He can manage with a broken shell for a little while. In fact, we're going to fix you *all* up.'

'What do you mean?' asks Teg.

'That contraption of yours,' says the chief. 'It wasn't exactly built for flying, was it?'

Teg crosses his arms and mumbles something incomprehensible.

'What are you going to do to it?' says Lippy, but the chief is busy staring at Cadno, his tail flicking solemnly back and forth, leaving a comet trail of sparks in its wake. Maybe being so close to a fire is making him miss his own flames.

'A firefox that has become an electrafox,' the chief says, more to himself than to anybody else.

'Oh no, I know that face,' says Albanact. 'He's getting an idea.'

'I do that face all the time,' says Lippy, with a knowing nod.

'Yes, very interesting . . .' says the chief, and then he snaps out of his daze and addresses us. 'Leave it to us snabbits. We'll sort it all out. Now, come on, off to bed.'

The chieftess creates a big nest for us all in front of the fire, using an assortment of blankets, pillows, cushions and throws. It's not exactly a bed, but it is by far the comfiest, cosiest set-up I have ever had the delight of nestling in.

'I can't stop twiddling my toes!' Roo sings. 'I always twiddle my toes when I'm toasty!'

'This is *so* much comfier than my queen-sized bed back at the palace!' Branwen beams.

We're all bundled up in various patches of the nest, the firelight dancing across our faces. Lippy declared early on that she wanted to make her sleepy snug next to Branwen's. ('Of course you do,' I murmured, exchanging pointed looks with Roo.) The rest of the burrow is in darkness now that the chief and chieftess have gone to bed, but the room still hums with homely night-time sounds – the sleepy *tick-tock* of the grand-father clock, the whispering crackle of the fireplace.

'You've got the best home ever, Albie,' says Lippy, lying on her belly with her chin cupped in her hands. Blodyn sits next to her, thawing out nicely before the fire. 'Why didn't you tell us how amazing snabbits are?'

Albanact, enveloped in colourful blankets, sighs. 'I was never as good as the other snabbits at fixing things. I used to get laughed at when I tried to wire up a pocket watch and it would start to go backwards instead of forwards. So I started to dream of leaving this place and building a new life for myself – a *better* life. I didn't want to stay in these hills like the rest of the snabbits, never getting credit for our creations. I wanted to do something *big*, something *amazing*.'

'Well, you're the Queen's Royal Advisor now,' says Teg, with a smirk.

Albanact's eyes widen. 'Yes, Your Majesty, about that –'

Branwen holds up a hand. 'We'll negotiate terms once this whole ordeal with Gawr is over. Right now, I want to enjoy the peace.'

'Fair enough,' says Albanact, and then his lips pucker at the corners.

'Albie, what are you doing to your *face*?' Teg frowns.

'I'm smiling!'

'Wait, is that your smile?' says Teg. 'It looks like you're trying to swallow a slug.'

'Oh, I don't know why I bother,' Albanact huffs.

'I'm just messing with you! It's nice to see you smiling, my friend. What's got you feeling happy?'

'I suppose I've just realized that snabbits aren't all *that* bad,' Albanact replies, turning to gaze at the fire.

'No, they're not,' I say. 'They're wonderful.'

Roo lets out a pained yelp. We all look over and spot him wriggling out of the snug he's made for himself, nursing his bottom. The baby crafanc's head pokes out after him, a blanket snagged on his bigger tusk. He licks happily at the air.

'This thing is doing my head in,' Roo mutters.

'You need to give that *thing* a name,' Lippy says sternly. 'He's imprinted on you now. You need to start looking after him properly. You've been moaning all trip about wanting something that's yours and only yours!'

'Yes, but I didn't mean a prickly loaf of bread with legs and teeth!'

Branwen laughs. 'He *does* look a bit like a loaf of bread.'

'Prickly,' I say thoughtfully. 'What's the Welsh word for *prickly*, I wonder . . .'

'It's *pigog*,' says Lippy. 'I hear Mum saying it all the time when people bring hedgehogs into the surgery.'

'Pigog,' says Roo, and the baby crafanc tilts his head like he's just heard something funny. 'I think that fits, don't you?'

'Welcome to the family, Pigog!' Lippy grins. 'Oh, he *is* quite cute, you know.'

Pigog makes a cooing noise and bats the blanket nest with his flipper tail. It looks like he's trying to convince Roo to cuddle back up inside. Roo obeys, dutifully sliding back into his snug and wincing as Pigog snuggles up to him.

'I suppose he is,' he mutters, but then his expression softens. 'He's definitely nice and soft – Ouch! *Apart from those blimmin' spines!*'

We all laugh, and even Roo can't help but snigger, albeit reluctantly, and soon after that we say our goodnights – not that it stops Lippy and Branwen from whispering and giggling long into the night.

'I wish one of them would hurry up and ask the other one out already,' Roo mutters, eyes drooping shut. I nod in agreement.

'What did you just say?' Branwen snaps from across the snug.

'Oh, nothing, nothing . . .' I reply slowly, my own eyelids growing heavy, and then I sink into sleep.

Chapter 18

Chief Cadwaladr has us up at the crack of dawn.

'Come on, up you all get!' he declares, marching into the living area with more energy than should be allowed at this time of day. 'It's time for breakfast, and then we're off!'

The chieftess herds us to the table in the kitchen, plonking plates piled high with pastries and toast in the middle for us to pick from. We're all still yawning, but we can hardly sit down fast enough, eager to get breakfast out of the way so we can set off for the mountain.

'First things first. Albie, I think it's best if you stay here today,' says the chieftess, 'what with your shell being in the state it is.'

Unsurprisingly, Albanact doesn't object.

'I'll stay behind, too,' says Teg. 'I want to see what Chief Cadwaladr has planned for the Fargone Falcon. Maybe I could learn a thing or two from the snabbits.'

We set off as the sun is still rising, casting a honeyed light on to the slopes of the hills. The ruins of the Fargone Falcon have disappeared overnight, but Chief Cadwaladr assures us that everything is in hand.

'Leave it to us!' he booms, and then he points in the direction of the mountains. 'Now, follow me. This way! Come on, chop-chop!'

The chief moves surprisingly fast. They may have snail shells on their backs, but that doesn't mean snabbits go slowly. We wind through the hills, passing more subtle entrances into the Warren, and eventually the land begins to slope upward more steeply towards the foot of the mountains.

The path to Cariad's Keep is treacherous. It doesn't take long for the slopes to turn to ragged trails cut through the rocks, and every now and then an ear-piercing crack seems to split the world in two as stones crumble from the mountainside and crash on to the path before or behind us. It makes Cadno's hackles rise, sparks fizzing up and down his body. Pigog hides inside Roo's jacket.

'You're definitely a softie, aren't you?' I hear him coo. 'No wonder you didn't fit in with the rest of the crafancs.'

I smile to myself, knowing that Roo is already starting to change his mind about his newfound animal companion.

After a while, as the path keeps twisting upward, flakes of snow begin to fall from the sky.

'Blodyn, is it you doing that?' asks Lippy, but the frostdoe shakes her antlers.

'No, I think it's *actually* snowing,' I say. We edge

round a ginormous rocky outcrop and, sure enough, the slopes and peaks before us are completely white. Not for the first time, I feel an ache for Cadno's missing fire. There's nothing comforting about electric sparks.

We struggle onwards. Cadno, who's never experienced proper snow before, bounds along the winding path, snapping at flakes and diving head first into thick drifts, so that only his bum and tail can still be seen. Pigog whizzes through the air next to him, batting snowballs at Roo with his tail.

'All I wanted was a peaceful life,' Roo groans, dodging a fresh snowball. It soars over his head and gets impaled on one of Blodyn's antlers.

'You actually did say you wanted a special friend of your own,' I remind him.

'Yes, I know,' Roo snaps. 'But I had something more, I dunno . . . *impressive* in mind.'

'Don't write him off, Roo,' says Lippy. 'Pigog might go on to do something brilliant one day.'

'Hmm,' Roo mutters as the baby crafanc gnaws at a dangling icicle. It snaps off in his mouth and Pigog turns, the icicle now hanging behind his shorter tusk, giving the illusion that he's got a full one.

'He's got a good sense of humour, at least,' I say as Pigog chases after Cadno, the two of them panting happily.

After what feels like hours of climbing, the slope evens out and we reach a basin beneath the peaks.

'Well, here we are,' says Chief Cadwaladr, his voice grave.

We stop on the crest of an incline. The scene before us must once have been a peaceful one, but now it's a picture of utter devastation. There's a vast lake, but the frozen surface has been shattered in places by boulders so enormous that they protrude from the water like jagged, toothy islands. The opposite shore, which is made up of the steep slopes of the peaks beyond, is riddled with enormous craters, and some of the mountaintops themselves look as though they've been flattened by a giant fist.

It's clear that a titanic battle has recently taken place here.

'Cariad's Keep is up there,' says the chief, pointing to the highest peak, but then he grimaces. 'Or, at least, it *was*.'

The top of the peak is splintered, as if somebody or some*thing* colossal has snapped it in half. Where Cariad's Keep was, there is now only a huge pockmark in the mountain.

'Gawr did all this?' I ask, gesturing at the destruction around us.

Chief Cadwaladr nods sombrely. 'There used to be a grotto near the top of Idris, where Llew the sunlion kept the Cariad safe. On a clear day, we snabbits could often see him weaving in and out of the mountains as he patrolled the peaks. As you can see, the grotto is no more.'

'Could you tell us again what happened?' Branwen asks.

'Gawr took Llew by surprise, just after sunset, otherwise the battle might not have been so one-sided,' says the chief. 'All we could see from below were rocks being hurled, mountaintops exploding, and the giant forms of Gawr and Llew colliding with each other. It was a terrible sight.'

'So Gawr defeated Llew and took the Cariad,' I say. 'But, then, where is Llew? What did Gawr do with him?'

We glance around, part of me fearful that we'll stumble across the sunlion's lifeless form, half buried in the snow. But, apart from the ruin that their battle left behind, there's no sign of Llew anywhere.

'There *must* be a clue here somewhere to show us what happened to Llew!' says Branwen, her face twisted in frustration. 'We can't just have come up here for nothing!'

'It's not like there's even any giant footsteps for us to follow,' says Lippy. 'They've all been covered up by the fresh snowfall.'

We begin our search, peering inside the snow-filled trenches and craters that Gawr's giant feet left behind. Pigog uses his flipper tail to bat entire drifts aside, but no matter how long or hard we seek, our mission proves fruitless.

Until Cadno starts barking. I turn, and what I see makes my stomach plummet down to my butt.

Cadno has wandered right out on to the frozen lake.

'Cadno, no!' I cry, running down to the shore. I step out on to the lake, but the ice cracks beneath my feet, and my friends grab me by the scruff of my neck.

'Charlie, you'll get yourself killed!' Lippy cries, tugging me away. Pigog scurries up on to Roo's shoulder and watches the scene unfold.

'But Cadno –' I stammer, but then my voice trails off. 'Wait, what is *that*?'

Cadno is standing on the ice about five metres away, staring down into the depths of the lake. He may still be a cub, but he's started shifting some of his puppy weight recently, his limbs elongating and his round belly turning to hard muscle. I just hope he's not heavy enough to break through the ice yet.

And he's *found* something. Because there, lying on

the bed of the lake, flickers something golden.

'I think I know what it is,' says Lippy, her face lighting up. She turns to her animal companion. 'Blodyn, can you help?'

Like Cadno, Blodyn has been a bit miffed with her swapped power. I guess she's missed being able to make flowers spring around her feet. But now she strides gallantly forward, her eyes narrowed in determination.

She marches out on to the ice, and I wince as her hoofs make sharp clacking sounds on the surface – but, of course, Blodyn is a frostdoe now. She's the *boss* of the ice. If she doesn't want it to break beneath her weight, it won't.

We watch as Blodyn reaches Cadno, the cub humming with electricity as he stares at the glimmer of gold on the lakebed. She leans down, sniffs tentatively at the ice, and then goes very still.

We wait, and a few seconds later the ice at their feet starts to crack. I tense, terrified that our friends are about to plunge into the chilly depths of the lake, but then I realize that this is Blodyn's doing. The ice splits, making a circular opening in the frozen surface, and a new pillar of ice starts to push up from the lakebed, with the golden object sitting on top of it.

It emerges from the water and Cadno gently clasps it between his jaws. He walks back over to us, and I take it from him, my heart fluttering as I realize what it is he's found.

A golden feather.

It's as long as my forearm, and shines as though it was plucked from the sun itself. Which must mean . . .

'Llew's feather,' I say. Then again, louder, more excitedly: 'This feather belongs to Llew!'

'It's *beautiful*,' Lippy breathes.

'I wonder if there are more?' says Branwen, glancing around. 'If he lost one feather, chances are he lost others! Maybe we can use them to track him down . . .'

As though in response, Cadno sniffs at the air and barks, before setting off at a sprint round the perimeter of the lake. We follow and find him digging at a mound of snow on the opposite shore. There's something sharp and shiny poking out of it.

The quill-end of another feather.

Cadno emerges from the hole with the second feather clamped delicately in his mouth, and trots proudly over to us.

'I was right! Another one!' Branwen sings gleefully. 'They seem to be heading in *that* direction.'

She points over the cusp of the closest peak, and so off we set once again, Cadno leading the way.

Within half an hour he's found three more feathers, one of them snagged on a rock high up on the mountainside, which Pigog soars up to retrieve ('See,' says Lippy, 'he *can* be useful!'), and the other two buried in the snow.

They all seem to be leading in the same direction . . .

'South-west,' says Chief Cadwaladr thoughtfully. 'Hmm . . . how curious.'

'What?' I ask.

'That's the direction of Gawr's prison,' says Branwen, her expression darkening. 'It could just be a coincidence, but something is telling me it's not.'

'Gawr's prison?' I repeat, my mouth falling open. 'Wait . . . do you think Gawr took Llew to his old enchanted dungeon and locked him inside?'

Branwen stares into the distance, her brows knitted together.

'I don't know,' she says, 'but there's only one way to find out.'

Chief Cadwaladr marshals us off the mountain before any of us can protest.

'No way are you going without any supplies!' he barks. 'You'll come back to the Warren, fill your coffers with food, and then off you go. Besides, I'm sure the other snabbits will have finished their work on your transportation by now.'

'Already?' Roo blurts.

'We may have snail shells, but never underestimate

the speed of the snabbit,' says Chief Cadwaladr, a proud glint in his eye. 'Once we get going, it's hard to stop us!'

It takes a few hours to get down off the mountain. By the time we get back to the Warren, my clothes are soaked through from snow and sweat. The chieftess gives us dressing gowns to change into and drapes our clothes before the fire to dry, and then Teg appears.

His eyes are bright with excitement, and when he starts talking, it's like his mouth can't keep up with his brain.

'Guys, you *have* to come and see what the snabbits have done. You won't *believe* it – they've transformed the Fargone Falcon. Come on!'

Chief Cadwaladr hoots with laughter as we're taken outside to the clearing where we crash-landed the day before. The carriage is back, only this time the hot-air balloon is nowhere to be seen.

And what a sight the carriage is to behold.

It's not just a carriage any more. Now it's some sort of carriage-aeroplane hybrid, with wings built on to

each side. It's surrounded by snabbits wielding various tools.

My mouth drops open. 'It's . . . it's . . .'

'It's *amazing*,' Branwen finishes, 'but, er . . . what is it?'

'This is the latest in transport technology,' says the chief. 'The likes of which has never been seen before in Fargone!'

'OK,' says Branwen uncertainly, 'but what *is* it?'

'A flying carriage!' says the chief. 'It will take you anywhere you want to go. The skies are its roads! And you won't have to worry about any silly balloons getting punctured by rogue crafancs.'

At that, Pigog squeaks guiltily and burrows his face into Roo's chest. Roo pats his head comfortingly.

'Amazing, isn't it?' says Teg eagerly. 'Tell them how it's going to work! This is the best part.'

'It's going to be powered by electricity,' says Chief Cadwaladr, his gaze lingering somewhere near my feet. Specifically . . .

'Cadno,' I blurt out. 'It's going to be powered by Cadno?'

The cub tilts his head and twitches his ears, a couple of excited sparks shooting from the tips.

'In the past we've never had enough electricity to power the prototypes we've created,' says the chief. 'Unfortunately, creatures with electric powers are particularly difficult to catch and tame. But when you lot turned up with a friendly electrafox, I knew it was the perfect opportunity for us to put our invention to the test. Follow me.'

He leads us inside the carriage, which now looks so new that you'd never guess it had almost been split in two a day earlier. Against one end is a steering wheel, and opposite it, on the other side of the carriage, is the engine, attached to something that looks a bit like a metal lead, not dissimilar to the one we use to take Cadno for walks back home.

'All you've got to do is loop this round Cadno's neck. Once he starts producing electricity, the wheels will turn and the carriage will move forward. After you've gained enough speed, you'll take off! When you're in the air, somebody needs to steer the aircraft, and that's it. If you want to go up, Cadno will need to produce more power. Likewise, if you want to go down, Cadno will have to produce less power. It's very simple!'

It *does* sound simple. Almost as easy as flying a plane in one of my video games.

'It's brilliant!' I say. Cadno starts running around

in rapid circles, unable to contain his excitement at the prospect of finally being able to put his new power to good use. Pigog joins in, swimming through the air above him, while Blodyn does a happy little prance on the spot.

'I miss the giant Branwen faces,' Lippy mutters, and the queen shoves her playfully on the shoulder. Lippy's cheeks turn pink.

'It's genius,' says Branwen. 'Flying carriages powered by electricity . . . who would have thought something like this could ever exist?'

'Actually, remember when I mentioned aeroplanes before?' I say, but Branwen just gawps at me. 'You know what? Never mind.'

'Here, take these sandwiches, and these blankets, and some water. Oh, and don't forget the fruit, and some home-made cupcakes in case you fancy something sweet, and –'

'Mother, I think they've got everything they need,' Albanact grumbles.

The chieftess straightens herself up. 'Don't you pout just because you've got to stay here, my boy!'

The snabbits have been so busy working on the new Fargone Falcon that they haven't had time yet to fix Albanact's shell, so it's been decided that he will stay behind while he gets patched up. To my surprise, Teg chooses to stay behind, too.

'What?' I ask in disbelief. 'But don't you want to fly in our new carriage?'

Teg bites his lower lip. 'Of course I do!' he exclaims, and then glances over his shoulder to where Albanact and his parents sit at the kitchen table, lowering his voice. 'But I can't leave Albie, can I?'

'He's with his family. He'll be OK.'

'I know that, but I'm as much his family now as they are,' Teg replies, with an air of fondness. 'He might be grumpy, but he's one of my closest companions.' From his shoulder, Kevin gives a reminding squeak. 'You too, Kevin. Obviously. Can't go anywhere without you two, can I? So, no. I'll stay here.'

He might be itching to take a ride in our new vehicle, but it's clear he isn't going to change his mind – and I admire him for that. I wouldn't leave Cadno anywhere, would I?

So that's how we come to be boarding the carriage for a second time, except this time we're setting off to a crowd of cheering snabbits instead of people.

'Oh, look, the snabbits have installed seatbelts!' says Roo. 'Finally, some sense!'

Branwen is the last to board and, just like she did the last time, she turns to address the gathering.

'Thank you, snabbits, for your hospitality!' she says warmly. 'And for extending your artistry to the Fargone Falcon and turning it into a magnificent flying vessel! Once this ordeal with Gawr is over, I will ensure that the whole of Fargone knows about your craftsmanship!'

The snabbits go wild, hopping and applauding, their ears bouncing up and down in a fluffy, churning tide.

'And rest assured, this ordeal with Gawr *will* end,'

Branwen goes on, 'for we are off to find Llew the mighty sunlion, and then we will blast Gawr and his fort from the sky and restore the Cariad to –'

She pauses as the snabbits all stop bouncing, a chorus of laughter coming from them instead. A few of them point, leaning in to chuckle with one another.

'They're laughing at me again,' Branwen mutters out of the side of her mouth. 'What's going on?'

Lippy leans round and peers into her face.

'Oh my.'

'What is it?' Branwen hisses.

'Googly eyes, B!'

'What? My eyes aren't googly!'

'No, B – there are googly eyes on your chin!'

Branwen whirls round to face me and Roo, turning her back on the audience. My gaze goes straight to her chin where, sure enough, there's a pair of googly eyes stuck to her skin, the black dots of the pupils jiggling about inside as her hands come up to swipe at them.

'*Googly eyes?*' she growls. 'Why are there googly eyes on my chin? How did they get there? Why is this happening again?!'

Next to me, Roo snorts.

Branwen shoots him a glare. 'Is something funny, Rupert?'

He freezes, jarred by her use of his full name. 'I, er . . . no . . . it's just that . . . well . . .'

'Come on, spit it out. I'm sure the rest of the group would love to be in on the joke.'

Roo looks down. 'Oh, it's nothing . . . it's just your chin looks like an upside-down smiley face now. It's funny.'

I tilt my head a bit, and suddenly I can see where he's coming from. If you covered the top half of Branwen's face, her chin *would* look like an upside-down smiley face. The effect is comical, but I don't dare smile, not when she looks so angry.

'Well, I'm glad you're having a laugh at my expense!' she spits, and then she picks the googly eyes off her face. They're just like the ones I imagine Albanact would have glued to his bunnyhood pine-cone collection.

'I must be cursed,' she starts muttering to herself. 'Why do things keep appearing on my face when I'm speaking in public? What's going on?'

'I don't know!' Lippy squeaks. 'It's all very strange! They're gone now, though. So just take a deep breath and turn back round. They'll forget about it in a few minutes.'

Branwen closes her eyes, her shoulders rising and falling as she inhales and exhales. 'You're right,' she says, with a strained smile. 'Thank you, Lippy.'

She gives Lippy's hand a squeeze, and then she turns back round.

'Apologies for that little interruption,' she declares, her voice as booming as it was before, as if there had never been googly eyes stuck to her chin at all. 'Where was I? Oh yes! We will blast Gawr and his fort from the sky and restore the Cariad to its rightful place, bringing peace and equilibrium to Fargone once again!'

Lippy was right about the crowd, at least. They forget about the googly eyes pretty quickly and instead go back to their cheering, their applause reaching an ear-piercing crescendo as Branwen enters the carriage, her smile vanishing and her eyebrows fusing together in annoyance.

'Close the door,' she grumbles. 'Let's get going.'

She heads to the steering wheel, having been given a detailed demonstration by Teg a few hours ago as to how it all works.

'Cadno, take your position,' I say.

Cadno lets out a willing bark, excited to finally be of use, and sits himself next to the engine. I loop the metallic lead round his neck, making sure it's not too tight, and then stand aside.

'Are we ready?' asks Branwen.

'Ready,' the rest of us say together. Blodyn taps her front right hoof once. Pigog does a single confirming somersault.

We're good to go.

We give the crowd a final wave through the

windows. I spot Teg, Albanact and the chief and chieftess standing at the front, cheering louder than anybody else. It makes my heart hum with determination. We have to save Fargone.

'It's time to unleash that inner fire, Cadno,' I say, and then smile. 'Or, in this case, your inner spark.'

Lippy grins. 'Light the spark, Cadno!'

'Power up, little one!' says Branwen, her hands firmly on the steering wheel.

Cadno closes his eyes and an outbreak of sparks ripples across his body. They travel up the lead and into the engine, which suddenly judders to life. The floor rumbles beneath our feet.

'It's working!' Branwen exclaims. 'More, Cadno!'

'Time to strap in!' says Roo, perching himself on one of the floor cushions and lacing a seatbelt round his waist. 'You too, Pigog.'

Pigog obliges with a disgruntled look on his face, tucking himself under the belt next to Roo.

Cadno starts to glow, his body illuminating like a light bulb, sending power up the wire and into the engine. The carriage begins to roll forward, wheels turning.

'You're doing it, Cadno!' I exclaim. 'Keep it up!'

And then we're moving faster and faster, until we leave the glade and the snabbits behind, the hills turning into a blur of green.

'*Yeeehawwwww!*' Branwen cries. 'Up we go!'

A funny feeling comes over me as we seem to become weightless, the world falling away beneath us. It's working. We're in the air.

We're on our way to find Llew.

Chapter 20

Electrafox power is by far the fastest mode of transport we've had. We soar over the hills, over the mountains we climbed this morning, and find ourselves above the scene of Gawr and Llew's battle just ten minutes after leaving the Warren.

'Keep an eye out for more golden feathers,' says Branwen, her gaze fixed firmly on the sky as she focuses on piloting the flying machine.

The feathers we found earlier are hanging from the steering wheel, a constant reminder of the task ahead.

Lippy, Roo and I rush to the windows and peer down at the ground as we race towards the last spot where we stumbled upon one.

'There!' Lippy cries, pointing to the shores of another frozen lake. I squint, and there it is: a flicker of gold.

'They definitely seem to be heading in the direction of Gawr's old prison,' says Branwen solemnly. 'Let's keep going.'

We keep flying, staying relatively low so that we can follow the trail of Llew's fallen feathers. We find them scattered in a line that goes on for miles as the landscape beneath us transforms from snowy and rocky to hills and fields and lakes. And as the snow thins, deep trenches that gouge the earth begin to appear, heading in the same direction as the path of golden feathers.

'Gawr's footsteps,' says Branwen, through gritted teeth. 'Heading back towards the prison he came from.'

'Look,' Lippy gasps, pointing. 'There are also

footsteps heading in the other direction, from when he escaped!'

She's right, I realize. A short distance away, we spot more footprints set into the earth, this time heading *towards* the Carreg Mountains.

'What's that?' asks Roo, pointing straight ahead, to a black scribble that's looming on the horizon.

'Rotwood,' Branwen replies. 'A forest full of things that creep and crawl and consume. It's not a very nice place. I guess my ancestors thought it a good place to put Gawr's dungeon. Alas, it's definitely not a good place for a sunlion.'

'Why?' I ask.

'Because this part of the country gets very little sunlight,' Branwen explains, 'and the sunlion *thrives* on sunlight. The mountains mean it's often rainy here, and Llew can't recharge if he can't bask in the sun.'

'A bit like the solar-powered fairy lights my pa bought for the garden,' I say, and I feel a pang of yearning. I know they think we're safe, but I still feel bad for misleading my dads.

And just as importantly, I hope *they're* OK, that the rain back in Wales has subsided, and that the dam is no longer threatening to burst. Somehow, I doubt that's the case, though. The goings-on here in Fargone feel inextricably tied to the freak weather that's happening back in Wales.

'Pardon?' Branwen blinks at me.

'Never mind.'

Rotwood looms closer, and after a few minutes I can make out the line of gnarled trees that marks its edge. We soar over the threshold of the decaying forest, and pretty soon there's nothing below us but crooked trees with twisting limbs draped in slimy curtains of moss, carpets of mulchy leaves and thorny brambles crowding at their roots.

It doesn't look like a very pleasant place.

We keep going for miles, a reel of endless dead forest passing below, one of us occasionally letting out an excited gasp as we spot another feather caught on a branch or tangled in some knotty roots. We stay low so that we can see through the mist, and every now and then the tip of a tree clips the underside of the carriage, as if trying to reach up and pluck us from the air.

There are areas where the trees have been completely crushed by the giant's passage, but there doesn't seem to be any sign of struggle from Llew.

'The chief said that Gawr carried Llew away, remember?' Lippy whispers, horrified. 'Llew must have been unconscious!'

Eventually we come to a clearing, and Branwen instructs Cadno to ease off the power. The electricity that has been coursing all over his body for the duration of the journey begins to dwindle, and the carriage starts descending.

I rush to the window and spot a trapdoor set into the forest floor. But this isn't the sort of trapdoor you might see on TV, hidden underneath a rug in an old, haunted mansion. This one is *enormous*, almost as big as the playground back at school. There's an open slot in the middle, the size of a swimming pool, with metal bars like the sort you'd find in a jail cell.

'Wow,' I say. 'Is that . . . ?'

'Gawr's prison?' says Branwen. 'Yep. Looks cosy, doesn't it?'

We touch down, and the moment the doors open, the ominous atmosphere of Rotwood creeps in. My nostrils fill with the smell of damp, decaying things, and the harsh *caw* of a crow pierces the air.

I remove Cadno's lead and bundle him into my arms. Roo does the same with Pigog, and Lippy and Branwen both stick close to Blodyn as we step outside. The sun has vanished, and a low-lying mist seems to engulf everything around us.

'I think they put him here so that he was far away from everything,' says Branwen. 'Plus, Rotwood is full of dangerous creatures, so it's less likely that somebody would sneak in to try and free him.'

Next to me, Roo gulps. 'D-dangerous creatures?'

'Don't worry,' says Branwen. 'We've got three very powerful companions right here to help us in case we bump into any trouble.'

On Roo's shoulder, Pigog farts and gives himself such a fright that he rolls off.

Roo wriggles his nose. 'Yeah . . . powerful.'

'So what do you think happened?' asks Lippy.

Branwen purses her lips. 'I don't know. There's a key, but that's kept safe at the palace . . .'

'But Gawr can't have broken free by himself, because the door is still intact, and he would have been too weak because of the enchantment, anyway,' I say. 'Somebody *must* have let him out. Branwen, do you think someone *stole* the key from the palace?'

Branwen grimaces. 'I just don't see how . . . the palace is so well protected,' she says, and then shakes her head. 'Come on, let's go check it out.'

We start making our way across the clearing, our feet sinking into the mulchy dead leaves, but then Branwen pauses.

'Look,' she says, pointing. 'Somebody *has* been here before us.'

I look across the clearing, and my heart sputters in terror at what I see: it's a giant spider, bigger than a car, crouched at the edge of the trees. I almost let out a scream – and Roo *actually* does – before I realize that it's not moving. In fact, its eight joyless black eyes look very much dead.

And that's when I spot it. A single arrow jutting from the beast's head.

'What *is* that thing?' Roo shrieks, his whole body racked by shudders of disgust.

'It's a twisterantula,' Branwen replies grimly.

I've never seen a twisterantula in the flesh before, but I recognize it from the illustration in Teg's magical-creatures encyclopaedia, and not for the first time I find myself wondering why on earth everything in Fargone is ginormous.

'Or, at least, it *was* a twisterantula. Hmm . . .'

'What is it, Branwen?' asks Lippy.

'Whoever killed this twisterantula must be the same person who released Gawr!' she says. 'But *how*? I just don't understand how they could have got their hands on the key. I've got a bad feeling about this . . .'

We approach the trapdoor, stepping on to it as

cautiously as if it was the frozen lake back at Cariad's Keep. I half expect a beast to blast through the wood beneath our feet, sending us flying through the air, but nothing quite so violent happens.

What *does* happen is that a groan sounds from the belly of the earth. It's a feeble sound, nothing like what I'd imagine coming from the mouth of the mighty sunlion, but it still makes us all pause.

'What was that?' Roo cries. He holds Pigog close, then yelps when one of the sharp plates on his back prods him in the chest.

Branwen doesn't answer, not at first. She keeps moving towards the barred window, and when she gets there, she leans down. We watch as she takes a deep breath and peers over the edge, into the pit of shadows beneath our feet. For a second, her expression betrays nothing, but then she smiles.

'Hello, Llew,' she says gently. 'We've been looking for you.'

We all join Branwen. I peek over the brink, and for a second I can't see anything.

But then something shifts in the darkness, and a face floats up towards us through the shadows.

Llew the sunlion is more beautiful than I'd ever imagined. He's huge, bigger than a shire horse. He's got the face of a lion, with bottomless amber eyes and a flowing mane that looks as though it once ran gold, but is now ashen, deprived of sunlight. I can't see them through the murk, but I can hear a flapping deeper down, which must be his wings unfurling as he climbs to get a better look at us.

This is the first time I've seen him properly, and yet I can already tell that he's a shadow of his former self, compared to what I saw in the tapestry back at the palace. His gaze, so ancient and wise, is heavier with sorrow than my heart can bear. The fur around his snout and his eyes is flecked with white, gradually turning paler the longer he spends in his underground dungeon, both the magic and lack of sunlight sapping him of life.

'Nice to meet you, Llew,' I say, leaning down so that my face is pressed through a gap in the bars. 'I'm

Charlie. This is Cadno. That's Roo, Pigog, Lippy, Blodyn, and the ruler of Fargone herself, Queen Branwen.'

The sunlion reaches up and presses his ginormous nose to my outstretched hand. It's bigger than a fully grown sunflower, but there's no moisture. Dad says that animals aren't quite right if their noses are dry.

'Oh, Llew, what did Gawr do to you?' asks Lippy, and the sunlion lets out a rumbling, mournful sound. I don't know if sunlions can cry, but it certainly looks like he's about to.

'How can we help when we can't understand him?' says Roo.

Just then, something astonishing happens. Cadno wriggles out of my arms and tiptoes his way across one of the bars, craning his neck so that his head almost disappears inside the dungeon. It makes me nervous that he might fall in, but there's no stopping him.

Cadno's and Llew's noses meet through the bars, and Cadno's ears prick up in that friendly way they often do. He's joined by Pigog, who flutters down to perch on a bar, and Blodyn, who elegantly picks her way across, despite having four spindly legs to worry about.

Llew makes another groaning sound, and then Cadno starts whimpering. Pigog lets out a horrified squeak, and Blodyn shakes her head in indignation.

'What are they doing?' asks Branwen.

'I think they're *talking*,' says Lippy, eyes wide with fascination.

They go on like this for a few minutes. Eventually, Llew growls and grunts and nudges his head at something, and our three animal companions lift their necks.

They go leaping across the bars until they reach the lock, which Cadno sniffs and then taps with his paw.

I hurry around the perimeter of the opening until I reach the lock. It's much smaller than you'd expect, small enough for a normal-sized key to fit into.

'Did Gawr lock Llew inside?' I ask.

Cadno barks in confirmation.

'So somebody *did* use the key to free him!' I exclaim.

'But *how*?' Branwen gasps. 'It's been kept safe at the palace all these years. How did somebody sneak in and steal it?'

At this, Cadno looks down.

'I don't think he knows the answer to that,' I translate.

'OK. Where is the key now?'

In answer to this question, the three animals indicate the sky: Pigog flies upward, Blodyn angles her head and Cadno swipes with his paw.

'Gawr has it,' I say, dread setting in. The mouths of

my friends drop open in dismay. If the giant still has the key, how on earth are we going to free Llew?

Branwen gulps. 'OK, well, there's only one thing for it. We're going to have to sneak into Gawr's fort and steal the key back.'

'Are you serious?' Roo asks. 'How are we supposed to sneak into Gawr's fort when it's crawling with crafancs?'

Pigog whimpers and zooms to hide behind Roo's back.

'Pigog, it's OK . . .' he says. 'I'm not going to let anything bad happen to you.'

'What choice do we have?' says Branwen. 'I know it seems impossible, but we also thought we wouldn't be able to defeat Draig.'

'Or the Grendilock,' I say. 'We've done lots of things we thought would be impossible.'

There's a fierce glimmer in Branwen's eyes. 'Exactly! What's one more impossible thing?'

I'm officially bolstered. I can feel the fire igniting

in my soul, the *sparks* zapping around my spirit.

'You're right.' I grin. 'We *can* do this.'

'That's all very well and good,' says Roo, 'but how?'

'Nope!' says Lippy. 'We're not going to be negative!'

'It's not negative to have a *plan –*'

'Llew, hold on just a little longer,' says Lippy. 'We'll be back soon to release you from this awful dungeon.'

Llew gives a low rumble, but then something in his expression switches. He goes from looking grief-stricken to wide-eyed in a heartbeat. He lets out a roar and swipes at the bars with his gigantic paws, making us all scream as they judder beneath us.

'Whoa, Llew, steady on!' I cry. 'We can't help it – we don't have the key!'

But then I hear something behind us, an unnatural hiss that makes the hairs on the back of my neck stand on end. I turn, and what I see will stay with me in my nightmares for a long time.

Llew wasn't getting angry or impatient with us. He was giving us a warning . . . about the very much *alive* twisterantula that's stepped out of the woods behind us.

Chapter 21

The monster steps past its dead friend and fixes us in its glare.

The nice thing about dead twisterantulas is that they don't move. Moving is sort of their thing, as we're about to find out. Because the live twisterantula never stays still: its legs spin and rotate, its whole body twisting and turning like a terrifying fairground ride. It snaps its jaws at us, spittle dripping down its fangs as it emerges from the margin of rotting trees.

'Oh dear,' I mutter.

I look over at my friends. Roo has turned green. Lippy and Branwen are clinging to each other for dear life. And the twisterantula is getting ready to pounce.

'I think now would be a good time to return to the Falcon,' Branwen squeaks.

'I agree,' I say, my own voice wobbly. 'Let's go. N-nice spidey . . .'

And that's when the monster leaps. It springs into the air, its legs rotating round its abdomen so that it soars towards us like some sort of spider-frisbee hybrid.

In a flash, we're all screaming and running for the Falcon as fast as we can. The spider lands just behind us and lets out a shrieking hiss, so shrill that it feels like it might burst my eardrums.

'Come on, Cadno!' I cry. 'Let's go!'

I don't pause to look back. I don't know if we'll be any safer inside the carriage, but surely it must be better than being out here.

I hear a spitting sound, and something white spurts over my shoulder and lands on the ground in front of me. It almost trips me up – a thick, elasticated band.

A *web*.

I pump my legs harder, Cadno sprinting next to me and Pigog zooming just above my right shoulder. But then I hear the spitting sound again, and Pigog gets plucked from the air and wrenched back.

'Pigog!' Roo screams, and we all come skidding to a halt, whirling round to face our enemy.

The twisterantula has reeled Pigog in on a strand of silk, and it's now turning the poor thrashing animal over and over between its pincers, like a spit-roasted piglet, slowly mummifying our new friend. Pigog squirms and squeals in terror, but it's no use. He's already wrapped too tightly. We stand there, gawping uselessly, as the monster prepares its next meal.

'Charlie, what are we going to do?' Roo shrieks, his eyes wild with panic.

I realize then that, despite one of our co-adventurers literally being the queen of the country, they all see me as their leader. I know the rest of this world thinks of me as Charlie the Legendary, but I always thought my friends still saw me as just . . . well, just Charlie.

But maybe I'm not *just Charlie*. Maybe I'm Charlie the Legendary for a reason, because during moments like this, terrible moments when somebody vulnerable is in danger, the fire within me flares up. The *spark*.

That's it! I think to myself. *All we need is a spark!*

'Cadno!' I command, pointing a finger at the monster. 'Use an electric attack! The biggest one you can!'

Cadno runs forward, a determined look on his face, and begins to charge himself up. Sparks flicker all over his body, and he radiates a zappy yellow glow. Then he closes his eyes, the sparks getting bigger and

brighter, until finally he unleashes a bolt of lightning that jolts through the air and hits the twisterantula square between the eyes.

The monster drops poor Pigog, who's now at least padded enough to not get hurt upon landing. A great dome of electricity envelops its body, its eight limbs locking rigidly. It lets out a screech, and then Cadno ceases his attack. The lightning disappears, and the twisterantula thuds to the ground, its body sizzling all over.

'Wow, Cadno,' says Lippy. 'That was . . .'

'Impressive,' says Branwen.

Cadno glances over at us, his tongue hanging from his mouth in a way that makes him look a bit self-satisfied. He's definitely finding his feet with this new power.

Roo hurries over to where Pigog lies on the ground, wriggling inside his silken cocoon. He looks like a giant marshmallow.

'Pigog!' exclaims Roo. 'I'm so glad you're OK!'

It takes us a while to free Pigog from his trap, but eventually we manage to loosen it enough that he can saw himself free using his spines. He rolls into the open arms of Roo, who picks him up and holds him close.

'See, you *do* care about him,' says Lippy, smugly.

'Of course I care about him,' Roo snaps. 'I'm not a total monster, you know.'

My friends laugh, and I reach down to stroke Cadno between the ears.

'You're doing a good job of being an electrafox, Cadno,' I say, and my best four-legged buddy leans happily into my hand. 'But I still think you were a better firefox.'

Just then, Llew groans from inside his prison. He must have been watching the whole incident unfold, powerless to help.

'I think he's telling us not to stick around,' says Lippy, casting her glance into the surrounding undergrowth, tendrils of mist curling from the line of dead and rotting trees.

'Llew's got a point,' says Branwen. 'Come on, let's not waste time. We've got a queendom to rescue. To the Fargone Falcon!'

'So how are we going to rescue the queendom?'

We're sitting inside the Falcon, having touched down on the outskirts of Rotwood. Everybody is still quaking from our close encounter with the twisterantula. Pigog hasn't emerged from Roo's jacket since we took off.

Branwen sighs. 'We need to somehow get the key from Gawr and then come back and free Llew.'

'Oh, *that* will be easy, won't it?' Roo mutters. 'What, are we just going to fly up, knock on the door and ask to borrow it?'

'Don't be ridiculous,' I say.

'*Me* being ridiculous?' Roo scoffs. 'Have you guys listened to yourselves? You're on about just wandering up to Gawr's fortress, like he won't capture us and turn us into jam or something!'

'We obviously won't use the front door!' Branwen snaps. 'We'll find another way in and hope we don't get seen.'

'Oh, yes, I'll keep my fingers crossed – that will do it!' Roo barks back.

'I know it's not much of a plan,' I say, 'but can you think of anything better? We *have* to get that key back.'

At that, Roo baulks and looks away. 'I guess not.'

'Well, there you go,' I say. 'We don't have much of a choice, do we? Let's rest here for a bit, and then it's onwards to Gawr's fortress.'

We're making a beeline directly for Cantre'r Awyr,

and it doesn't take long for what remains of the sky town to appear. We start passing beneath the odd hamlet being held aloft by great black swans that glide gracefully around, their midnight down dappled with swirls of galactic purple and speckles of starry white. They've each got a white moon shape on their forehead.

'Starswans,' says Branwen, 'They use their power to keep Cantre'r Awyr in the air. Or, at least, they used to.'

We whizz past a cottage floating on top of a rock. A starswan patrols around it, but there's something different about its feathers compared to the others'. They're still black, but the tips are tinged with green, like it's gradually changing colour.

Or like its power is slowly changing, I realize in horror. The magical imbalance that has had Fargone in its grip since the Cariad was stolen by Gawr is still spreading.

I watch as the starswan suddenly dips, dropping just a few metres, before righting itself again, with an alarmed squawk. The floating cottage trembles, and I notice a man and a woman stepping through the doorway, the man carrying a suitcase and the woman sniffling into a hanky.

It's only a matter of time before their beautiful home falls to the ground.

'How are they going to get down from there?' asks Lippy, her nose pressed against the window. 'Can't we help them?'

'We don't have time,' says Branwen, and I can tell the words pain her. 'But look! They've got parachutes!'

She points, and, sure enough, both the man and the woman have bulky backpacks on. Still, the thought of having to jump from all the way up here makes me feel queasy.

We keep flying, passing more and more houses, the starswans becoming fewer and fewer the closer we get to Gawr's fortress. There are definitely more houses down on the ground than there are left in the sky. There are ruins dotted all over the place: some in the middle of fields, others flattening patches of trees, and others jutting from the shores of the lakes that they made room for in the first place.

We stop in a valley for Cadno to rest just as Gawr's fortress comes into view. It's a terrible blight in the sky, four stark wooden walls and an arched doorway you could fit ten double-decker buses through. It floats above everything else, swarmed all over by adult crafancs carrying pieces of wood to the parts that are still under construction.

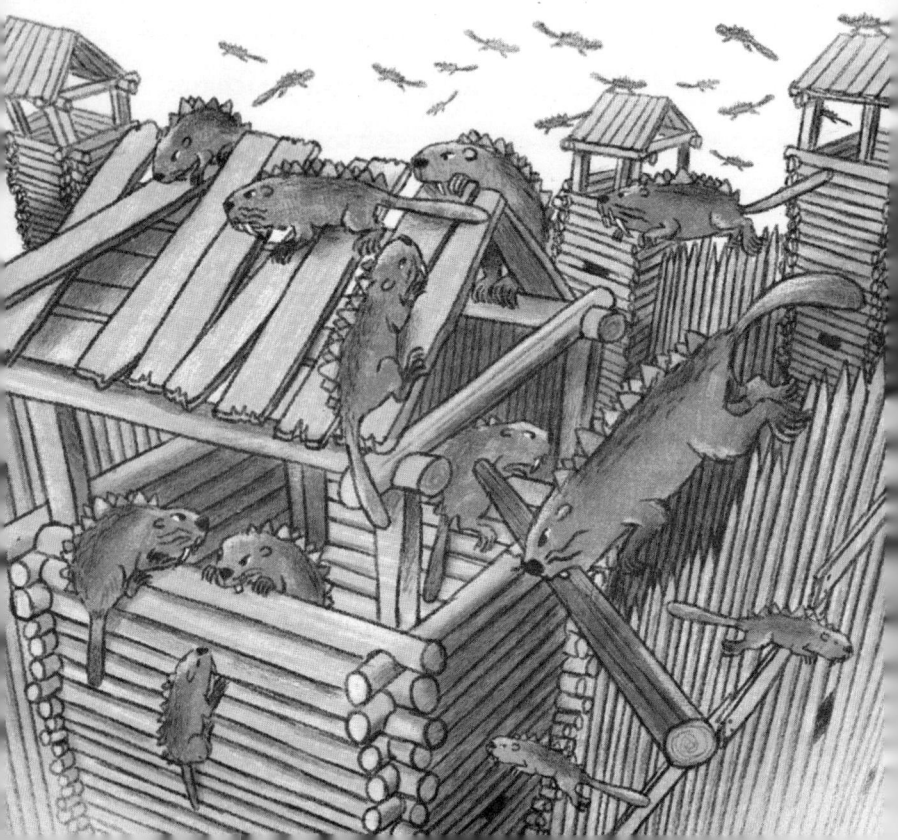

'Giants have no imagination,' Branwen says, with a sigh. We've landed behind a copse of trees, where hopefully neither Gawr nor his accomplices will spot us.

'I could have told you that as soon as we heard his poem,' says Roo.

'I mean, look at that,' she says, gesturing at the fort-in-progress. 'Look at how dull it is. It's completely lacking in character.'

'Would you say it doesn't *capture the essence* of Gawr's spirit?' asks Lippy, with a cheeky grin.

Branwen rolls her eyes. 'I was hoping never to hear those words again,' she says, and then she pauses. 'Actually, maybe it *does* capture the essence of Gawr's spirit – big and stupid!'

'It's the perfect fort for him!' I say, and then we're all laughing.

It feels strange for us all to be laughing together, considering what we're about to do. I can't help feeling that we're just putting off the terrible task that lies ahead. Because somehow, we now have to sneak into Gawr's headquarters and steal back the tiny key which he's *probably* got on his person somewhere. It's not like he's going to have a giant hallway table tucked just inside his giant doorway with a giant bowl to chuck his keys in when he gets home from a busy day of gianting, is it?

Our laughter trails off as the reality of what we're about to do hits home, and then the sound of distant thunder rolling across the land makes us look up.

'That's odd.' Branwen scowls. 'There isn't even any cloud!'

But then the ground starts vibrating. Ever so slightly at first, a tremble that fades and then comes back. It grows and it grows, the vibration getting stronger with every pulse, until it feels like Fargone has a case of the hiccups. The trees shudder around us, birds shooting from the canopy and forest creatures darting from the bushes as they flee whatever's coming.

'W-what is that?' asks Roo, holding his free hand out to steady himself.

'Something *big*,' says Branwen. 'And there's only one thing I can think of that's big enough to make an earthquake like this . . .'

'A *giant*,' I say, just as a shadow blots out the sun.

We look up as the biggest creature I've ever seen steps into the head of the valley. It's different seeing a giant from the ground. From the sky, they looked almost comical. From down here, there's absolutely nothing funny about them at all.

This one is shaped like a person, with two arms and legs, just like us, but I can't call him a human because of his sheer monstrousness. He stands taller than the upper slopes of the valley, as though he could simply bend his neck and bite chunks from the peaks like they're made of ice cream.

And then there's his face, his features marred and twisted with hatred. A big, knobbly nose that looks like it would flood a village with snot if he sneezed, and heavy brows that meet in the middle. He's got a mouth full of too many yellow teeth, all competing for space, some of them protruding over his lips.

'Is that Gawr?' Lippy cries.

'No, Gawr is even bigger,' says Branwen, eyes wide. 'That's a different giant. And it looks like he's not alone!'

Another giant steps into the valley behind the first. This one is a woman, with hair so long and dirty that there are entire trees tangled in it. And then behind her is another, this one with hunched shoulders, as though its bones can't handle its own tallness, and behind that another, and another, until, to my utter horror, the valley has filled with giants.

And they're heading directly for us.

They're all carrying uprooted trees as easily as bunches of flowers, or chunks of stone that they must have ripped from farm buildings. They've been out collecting material to be added to Gawr's fortress, I realize.

'Guys, I think we should move,' says Lippy, who's already slowly backing towards the Falcon. 'We're going to get flattened if we stay here!'

She's right. Each enormous step is bringing them

closer to where we're cowering. There must be over a dozen giants now, and they're already wreaking havoc wherever their feet land: gouging trenches, levelling trees, crushing boulders to dust.

We need to move, *now*.

We race back to the carriage and burst through the door, Cadno already hurrying for the engine.

But then we stop in our tracks, Lippy letting out a startled cry. Because there's something standing inside that wasn't there when we left a few minutes ago. Something tall and purple and fluffy that fills the already cramped space.

It's the grizzlarth.

Chapter 22

'Argh!' I exclaim. 'What are *you* doing here?'

The grizzlarth just stands there, rubbing a big paw over the new clock face on his belly, wearing a goofy expression.

'H-how did you –' Branwen stammers. 'Wait, did you teleport here?'

She looks utterly bewildered. I feel the same, to be honest.

The grizzlarth shrugs.

Branwen takes a deep breath. 'OK, my brain hurts,

but now is not the time. Grizzy, it's good to see you, but we've got to go. We've got a procession of giants to outrun.'

I nod in agreement. As much as I want to understand how the grizzlarth is here, now isn't the time. The ground is shaking violently underfoot, the giants approaching with every humongous step.

'Cadno, let's go!'

Cadno races to the engine and waits while I loop the metal lead round his neck, which is much harder when the whole world is trembling, and then he sparks up. The carriage judders to life and starts moving forward, with Branwen taking the wheel, and in just a few seconds we're climbing into the air once again.

'Phew,' says Lippy. 'At least the sky isn't shaking.'

'No,' says Roo from the window, 'but that doesn't make it any safer. Look!'

Lippy and I hurry over just as a huge shadow swings by, thicker than the thickest tree trunk, followed by another on the other side of the carriage.

Oh dear. They've caught up with us.

'We're between a giant's legs!' I cry. 'Branwen, watch out!'

Branwen quickly steers to the left, sending us all flying across the carriage with a chorus of screams. The grizzlarth knocks all the air out of me as he sandwiches me against the wall, smothering me in the fluff of his belly.

But then Branwen is veering to the right, and we go flying to the other side. This time, it's the grizzlarth's turn to cushion *my* fall. I risk a glance out of the window, and what I see makes my stomach flip over.

We're *surrounded* by giants. They're walking directly over the top of us, forming a tunnel with their legs that cuts off the light of the sun. If we get clipped by one of them, we'll be smashed to smithereens, and no amount of Cadno's lightning will be able to help us.

'Buckle up!' Branwen cries. 'This could be a bumpy ride!'

'Not again!' Roo wails, as he straps himself and Pigog into the seatbelts.

And then something collides with the back of the carriage. We lurch forward, but the force isn't enough to cause any real damage. I look out of the window again and my blood runs cold when I realize what it was that hit us.

It was a giant's *foot*. One of them *kicked* us.

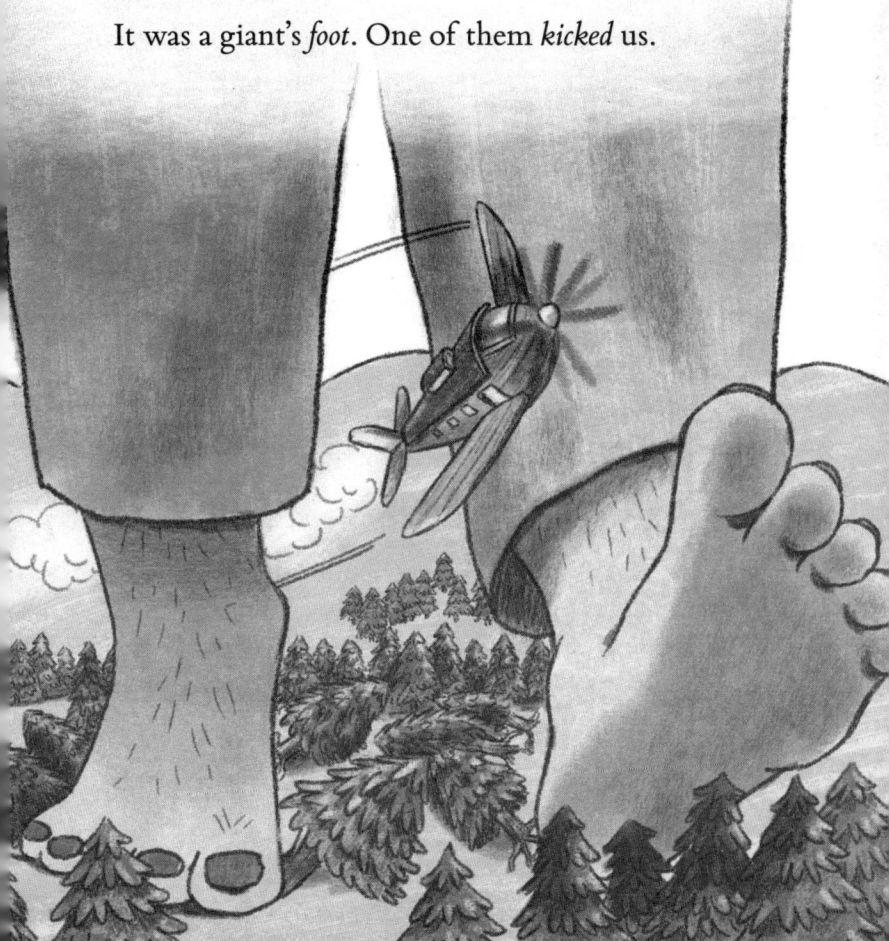

But it doesn't end there. Another enormous, booted foot comes hurtling towards us, and with it a booming sound of laughter, like an avalanche across the sky.

They're *laughing*. They're having fun – and at the expense of our lives!

'They're playing football with us!' I scream, just as the next foot is about to strike. 'Hold on tight!'

Everybody clings to whatever surface they can – Roo and Pigog to their seatbelts, Lippy and Blodyn to the handle of a cabinet, Branwen to the steering wheel, Cadno and I to the pipes of the engine. We're all waiting. I close my eyes, preparing for the final blow, the one that will shatter us to pieces.

But it doesn't come.

I open my eyes and, somehow, we're all still here. Did the kick miss? I glance out of the window, nervous of what I might see.

The giant looming over us is standing very still. I press my face against the glass so I can get a better look. It's not moving a muscle — not blinking, not breathing, its mouth frozen in dumb glee.

I look in the other direction and spot another giant, this one in a similarly motionless state.

'They're not moving,' I say, even as we continue to whizz by.

Branwen peers over her steering wheel. 'Is this part of their game?'

'I don't think so,' says Lippy, pointing out of the window. 'Look!'

We hurry to her side of the carriage, and when I spot what she's pointing at, my brain threatens to explode from the ridiculousness of it all.

It's a bird, flying not too far away as it tries to escape the chaos being caused by the giants.

Except, it's not actually flying. Its wings are poised mid-beat, but the bird itself is still, suspended in the air like a piece of fruit hanging in jelly.

The only thing that seems to be still moving is us.

'I don't understand,' I say. 'It's like time has stopped for the whole world, apart from . . .'

I trail off when a chuckling sound comes from behind us. We turn in unison, and that's when I finally understand what's going on. The grizzlarth stands in the corner of the carriage, his head bumping against the roof, trailing a fluffy paw over the clock-face pattern on his belly.

'Wait, *that's* your power?' I gawp. 'Teg thought you could teleport, when really you can stop time?'

The grizzlarth's belly jiggles up and down as he laughs. He's clearly very pleased with himself.

'What, just like that?' asks Branwen. 'Your new power means you can just freeze time, then restart it again?'

The grizzlarth nods.

'Wait a minute,' says Lippy. She's got that look on her face that she gets whenever she's pieced parts of a puzzle together in her head. 'You've been following us this entire time, haven't you?'

'Can you explain in simple terms, please?' asks Roo.

'Don't you see? The grizzlarth has never been far behind us this whole expedition. He's even popped in to leave us a clue once or twice. Making impossible things happen while time's been standing still.'

'If you're saying what I think you're saying . . .' says Branwen, throwing her head back in a groan as the grizzlarth reaches into his fur – which is dense and fluffy enough to store all manner of secrets – and pulls out what I think at first is a bag of frogspawn, but which upon closer inspection appears to be a bag of . . .

'Googly eyes!' I cry. 'It was you! You froze time and painted a moustache on Branwen, and then you did it again and put googly eyes on her chin!'

The grizzlarth seems very proud of himself, hands crossed over his chest as he basks in the glory of his trickery.

'You made me look like a fool!' Branwen spits. 'If I was a nasty queen, I would have your head!'

The grizzlarth's eyes widen in fear.

'But I'm not,' she finishes, pointing her nose into the air. 'Luckily, I'm a nice queen, and I can now look back on the incidents with a sense of humour.'

The grizzlarth's shoulders sag with relief.

'So have you just been stopping time every now and then to keep up with us?' I ask, and the purple bear nods.

I return to the window, remembering that while the rest of the world has stopped, we're still moving. We've left the stomping giants behind, frozen in place like statues, and now we're soaring over the valley. I can see leaves suspended in mid-air as they flutter to the ground, and waterfalls that no longer cascade, awaiting the moment that time starts back up again.

And that's when the idea occurs to me.

'How long do we have until time starts again?' I ask.

The grizzlarth points to the clock face on its belly, where I notice a hand slowly ticking anticlockwise. It's currently at number eleven but counting down with every passing second.

'We have until the hand gets back to twelve,' says Lippy. 'Hard to believe we didn't realize this before, isn't it? I mean, it's literally got a *clock* on its belly.'

'We don't have time to focus on the past,' I say. 'We

have to focus on the present. And right now, we have a key to steal.'

'Charlie, what are you saying?' asks Roo.

'I'm *saying* that the grizzlarth has given us a chance,' I reply. 'What better way to sneak into a fortress full of giants than when time is frozen? We'll be in and out without Gawr even knowing we've been there!'

'That is *brilliant*!' says Branwen, slipping back into captain mode and returning to the steering wheel. 'Come on, no time to waste!'

And just like that, we've got a plan. We climb higher and higher, heading directly for Gawr's fort. It's higher than any of the remaining buildings of Cantre'r Awyr and, even trapped in time, it looks more terrifying the closer we get.

What it lacks in imagination, it makes up for in size. It is, quite simply, gargantuan. Four walls with a turret at each corner, and an arched gateway with a spiked portcullis. The portcullis is closed, but the gaps between the bars are so big that the Falcon will be able to slip right through.

Pigog squeaks as the fortress looms, and dives behind Roo's back. I'm about to ask what's spooked him when an ominous shadow floats by the window. I crane my neck to get a good look at it, and what I see fills my belly with dread.

It's an adult crafanc. Whereas Pigog is small and cute, the grown-ups are anything but. They're big, this one approximately the size of an alligator, covered in spiky brown fur and with plates on their backs that are purple around the edges and an angry red in the middle. Some have big chunks missing, as though another crafanc has sunk its tusks into them during a fight.

'Don't worry, Pigog,' says Roo protectively. 'They can't hurt you any more.'

Pigog peers round his companion, eyes wide and scared. Roo reaches down and holds him tight as we pass through a gap in the portcullis, the bars floating by on either side of the carriage, and then we're in.

We're inside Gawr's fortress.

Chapter 23

It's a good thing that time is frozen, because the inside of Gawr's fort is crawling with crafancs. They're laying floorboards, constructing tables, and a few are even hanging up photo frames on the walls of Gawr's vast hallways. We would never have been able to sneak in normally.

'Giants have no taste,' Branwen mutters in disgust as we soar by a painting of a particularly ugly one using an uprooted oak tree to do bicep curls. 'Look at how vain he is.'

'Says the girl who had an entire roomful of portraits tucked away in her palace,' Roo teases.

'And I despised each and every one of them!'

'Do you think that's Gawr?' asks Lippy as we hurtle down the hallway, passing more paintings of the same giant in various poses: flattening a charming village with his feet, jumping up and down in a lake as though it was nothing more than a puddle, using the side of a mountain as a punchbag. In each scene, the giant in question looks extremely pleased with himself, his knobbly features twisted into what I think is supposed to be a smile.

'I guess we'll find out soon enough,' I say.

'What are we going to do when we find him?' says Roo. 'We don't even know where he's keeping the key.'

'I'll know it when I see it,' says Branwen, and then, to our surprise, Pigog bursts from his hiding place and joins her at the steering wheel. He does an excitable cartwheel and seems to use his oval flipper tail to point.

'What is it, Pigog?' asks Roo. 'Do you know where to take us?'

The baby crafanc does a little somersault.

'Of course!' Lippy exclaims. 'This is where Pigog lived before he was exiled. He must know where Gawr keeps the key!'

'Wait a minute,' says Roo. 'What if Pigog knows where the Cariad is? We could steal it back right now and put an end to this whole ordeal!'

The crafanc dips his head.

'I don't think Pigog knows where the Cariad is,' I say. 'Gawr is hardly going to leave it lying around, is he? We need to grab the key and go. We're running out of time.'

I point at the grizzlarth's belly, where the hand is just approaching six o'clock. It's going down fast. If we don't hurry, we'll still be inside Gawr's fortress when time starts back up. That would be *bad*.

'If we do, can't you just freeze it again?' Roo asks the bear, but then he shakes his head and feigns a yawn.

'Maybe freezing time makes him tired,' says Lippy. 'He probably needs time to recharge!'

The grizzlarth nods in confirmation. I think of how many times we've had to stop during our flight just to let Cadno rest for a few minutes. And it must be even more tiring keeping time itself still.

We keep going, with Pigog guiding Branwen on which way to go. Left, right, left, left, right, until finally we emerge into a huge hall, so tall that the ceiling is a dot above us.

And sitting in the centre of the room, on an enormous throne, is the giant from the portraits. Bigger than any of the other giants by a long shot, his eyes and his nose and his lips are even more twisted and marred by his own cruelty, his hair longer and greasier. Everything about him is greater, more terrible, right down to the yellowed teeth and the skeletons of animals that have long since perished in the tangles of his manky beard.

It's Gawr. Even frozen, he's utterly terrifying.

I gulp. He's our biggest adversary yet. Bigger even

than Draig was. I can see now why Llew struggled to defeat him. How is *anybody* meant to beat something so gigantic?

'Phwoar! He's big, isn't he?' says Roo, and we all stare at him.

'Yes, Rupert, the King of the Giants is big,' Branwen replies. 'Now, quiet. Pigog needs to focus. Show us where he keeps the key, little one.'

Pigog swipes his flipper and guides us closer, each of us shrinking down further the nearer we get, petrified that Gawr is about to spring back to life and crush us all between forefinger and thumb.

I glance at the grizzlarth. The hand on the clock is fast approaching three now. I swear it's counting down faster. In fact, the magical bear *is* starting to look a bit tired, his brows furrowed in concentration as he works to keep time frozen.

'We need to be quick,' I say, urgency setting in.

'There!' Branwen exclaims, pointing.

I spot it. From a metal ring attached to Gawr's belt hangs a tiny silver key. It's so small compared to everything else in this fortress that it looks out of place, but there's no mistaking it.

We fly close enough that I could reach out of the window and pluck the key from its ring if it wasn't secured by a metal chain. My heart sinks.

'What are we going to do?' I hiss.

Pigog makes a determined trumpeting sound and flutters out of the window, veering so close to Gawr that they could almost touch.

'Pigog, no!' Roo exclaims. He hurries forward, but I put my hand on his shoulder, holding him back.

'Wait,' I say. 'Let him do his thing. Look!'

Sure enough, Pigog is *gnawing* at the metal ring, sawing away with his one good tusk. It takes a while, but eventually metal scrapings start to flick to the ground. I keep an anxious eye on the grizzlarth's clock, which has ticked down from three to two, and is now touching one.

We haven't got long left.

'Come on, Pigog,' I urge. 'You can do it.'

And then, just like that, the metal snaps. We jump in triumph as the key slides off the end, Pigog flipping around so that it falls on to his tusk. The baby crafanc returns to us and presents it to Branwen, who pats him proudly on the head.

'Excellent job, Pigog!' she sings, holding the key up high like a trophy.

Pigog bats at the air with his flipper. *No biggie*, he seems to be saying.

'Pigog,' Roo says, with a sense of awe. 'I had no idea you could be so . . . so . . . *useful*.'

Lippy grins. 'I told you!'

We don't waste another second. We turn and race from the throne room just as the clock hand starts counting down the final seconds of timelessness. We shoot through the passageways that lead to the front gate, and then we're bursting out and into the sky just as the hand on the grizzlarth's belly reaches twelve.

The crafancs leap back to life, swarming all over Gawr's castle without a clue that we've just broken its defences.

But as we're surging away from the fortress, the whole world shuddering back into motion, a howl full of rage rampages after us, shaking the very sky through which we flee.

Chapter 24

'We've got the key! We've got the key!'

We're all shouting, jumping up and down as we land deep in a valley, this one giantless. The grizzlarth has slouched in the corner, a look of exhaustion on his face, and Cadno is ready to collapse.

'That was *such* a close call!'

'Good job, Cadno, Pigog and Grizzy!'

We settle in a glade surrounded by trees, and the moment the carriage comes to a standstill, my little fox friend curls up for a power nap. The grizzlarth is already snoring, and it doesn't look like there'll be any waking him for a while. At least Cadno can recharge fairly quickly, but it must be even more draining having to freeze time across an entire queendom.

Our celebrations are cut short by the sound of Gawr's furious roar thundering down from the sky. He sounds very, *very* angry. Perhaps even angrier than Pa was when Cadno did a poo in one of his slippers.

Roo's cheeks pale. 'What do we do now?'

'We go back and release the sunlion,' I say, brandishing the key. 'Then we can end Gawr's rebellion once and for all.'

Branwen shakes her head. 'You need to be the one to go and free Llew, Charlie.'

I blink. 'Me?'

'Yes, you. We can't all go, can we? Llew is big, but he won't be able to carry us all back, and Cadno is already tired from powering the Falcon.'

I glance down at him, bundled in a sleepy ball. She's right. Cadno is almost spent. I vow to get him a snack in a few minutes.

'Let him rest for a bit, then you take the Falcon,' says Branwen, her official queen-voice taking over. 'Release Llew, then you and Cadno fly back on the sunlion.'

I gulp. 'OK, yeah. Just gonna casually ride a legendary sunlion. No biggie. Like riding a bike.'

'Don't forget, the dungeon is enchanted to weaken the prisoner,' Branwen reminds me. 'As soon as you turn the key in the lock, that enchantment will break. Llew won't be back to full strength straight away, but he should gain enough to blast free and fly.'

'You can do this, Charlie,' says Lippy.

I nod. Because I've learned by now that even when the prospect of something fills my stomach with worms, that doesn't mean I can't do it. Sometimes being scared is good. You can use fear as a fuel to ignite the spark in your soul.

I lean down and pat Cadno behind his ear.

'What do you think, boy?' I ask in a soothing voice. The fox winks one eye open. 'Do you think you've got one more flight left in you?'

He licks at the air, which I think means yes.

'Good boy. Rest up for a few minutes, and then we'll go. It's time to make you a firefox again.'

The rest of the Adventure Squad decide to keep a low profile by tucking themselves away in the forest where Gawr won't be able to see them. The sky around his fortress is already crawling with crafancs, who seem to be scanning the ground in search of the missing key. I make the gang promise that they'll stay hidden while I get the Falcon ready.

'We'll be fine,' Branwen assures me. 'Now, off you go. You've got a lost sunlion to free.'

Cadno has perked up after a short sleep, a snack of corned beef and a drink of water. The grizzlarth, however, doesn't look like he's going to wake any time soon. Roo gives him a polite prod to the belly, but the bear just growls and rolls over.

I gulp. Seems like the grizzlarth is out of action indefinitely.

'OK, I'd best get going,' I say, taking a deep breath. 'Cadno, are you ready?'

Cadno stands to attention, snout pointed gallantly into the air.

'All right, come on.'

We make our way into the carriage.

'Don't draw any attention to yourselves,' I call back to my friends.

'We could say the same to you,' says Lippy, who's holding Branwen's hand tightly.

I smile nervously. 'Bit hard. I'm in a flying, electrafox-powered aircraft.'

'Fair point.'

'I'll see you soon,' I say. 'I'll try not to be long.'

'Just make sure you come back with Llew,' says Branwen. 'It's time to put an end to Gawr's nonsense.'

Flying at full speed means we get to Llew's prison fast. It feels as though this day has lasted forever, but I remind myself that time was stopped for a large portion of it. We land next to the trapdoor, as far away from the motionless, many-legged twisterantulas as we can manage. They're still there, slumped on the ground, and very much dead – but that doesn't make them any less creepy.

Llew grumbles from inside his prison, like he's checking who we are.

'It's me,' I whisper. 'Charlie.'

Behind me, Cadno snorts.

I roll my eyes. 'And Cadno.'

I peer through the bars and into the shadows below. Even though the sun struggles to pierce the constant cover of mist, there's still enough light for me to see the sunlion craning his head towards the bars. He seems to have paled even more since we saw him just a few hours ago. I have no idea how the beast before me is meant to defeat Gawr, but I know I have to trust and believe.

The sunlion's eyes sparkle with recognition when he sees me. I lean close to the bars and our noses touch. He may be a shadow of his former self, but I can feel the power rising from him like steam.

'I've got the key,' I say, holding it up.

Llew's gaze flickers to it, and instantly he uses an enormous paw to swipe at the bars.

'You got it,' I say, and then I hold the beast's gaze. 'Are you ready for your freedom? Are you ready to face the monster who did this to you and return Fargone to its former glory?'

It sounds like something Branwen would say, but it feels good rolling off my tongue. At some point since becoming Cadno's guardian, I've gone from being a trembling mouse, scared of everything and anything, to a less-trembly mouse, still a bit scared of some things, but much more able to stand up to the nasty giants of the world.

I've got the spirit of a firefox flowing through my veins. And, in just a few moments, I'll have the roar of a sunlion to call my own.

A hero is nothing without his team. His human friends, his animal companions.

I, Charlie the Legendary, am nothing without the Adventure Squad.

And now it's time to welcome another member.

'I free you, Llew!' I cry, feeling a bit like I'm in a film, and then I ram the key into the lock and twist. I feel it click, and I know I've done my job.

I hurry back on to solid ground and turn, holding Cadno close to my chest, remembering what Branwen said about the dungeon's enchantment breaking as soon as I unlock it.

Seconds pass, and nothing happens. Did I not turn the key enough? Or worse – is it the *wrong* key?

I frown. 'Llew –'

A *CRACK* cleaves the air as the trapdoor explodes in an upward blast, wood and metal flying everywhere. I scream and turn to protect Cadno with my body, but luckily we avoid getting hit by any debris. We both peer back, and what I see might just be the most magnificent scene my eyeballs have ever witnessed.

Llew the sunlion is rising into the air, bigger than I had ever imagined him, with the hind talons and wings of an almighty eagle, each beat carrying him higher and higher into the sky. He tears a hole through the mist, rising to the sunlight that shines above, and

I watch in amazement as he starts to glow, the brilliant light enveloping his entire body.

I stare up at him, my heart pounding so hard I can feel it in my throat. The strength is returning to him, the light settling back into his mane, his feathers. But then the sun disappears behind a cloud, and the cocoon of light fades away. Llew descends, not quite as mighty as the image from the tapestry, his recharging cut short by the cloud, but still glorious – and utterly terrifying. I've never been this close to a lion, not even at a zoo, and yet here I am, standing mere metres from not just a lion, but a lion and an eagle mashed together.

As though he senses my nerves, Llew dips his head in greeting. He's showing me he's a friend, not a foe. He's not going to eat me.

'N-nice to meet you, Llew,' I say. I watch as Cadno strides forward, their noses just about touching, eyes closed as they welcome each other.

'Huh. That's much better than sniffing the other animal's butt like you'd usually do to say hello, Cadno.'

Cadno glances over his shoulder at me with the fox equivalent of an eye-roll. Llew leans down so that his front is angled closer to the ground, and Cadno scurries up his foreleg until he's perched on the sunlion's back, in the space between his wings.

I gawp up at him before meeting Llew's gaze. I swear, in that moment, he *winks* at me.

Oh, wait . . . is he a *sassy* sunlion?

'You want me to get up there, too?'

Llew growls, full of deep resonance, and nods.

'O-OK, but how am I supposed to – ARGH!'

I let out a scream when Llew reaches down with his left wing, scoops me up into a feathery bundle, and deposits me on his back alongside Cadno. It happens so quickly that I barely have time to register it.

But then I'm next to my best friend, and we're on the back of the legendary sunlion, and, in that moment, I feel invincible.

Llew roars, and I can feel the sound humming up from his body and into mine.

'Let's go, Llew!' I cry. 'Let's go and show that stupid giant who's boss – ARGH!'

For the second time in just a few moments, I scream. Because Llew has leaped into the air, and now Cadno and I are clinging on for dear life as he soars up, up, up. The world falls away, the air rushing at our faces, my stomach doing cartwheels.

We're off.

Chapter 25

Riding Llew is a nail-biting experience, to say the least. There's very little for me to hold on to, so I have to cling to his mane. If the sunlion feels a tug, he doesn't show it. And he flies with such power that I feel like I might fall off any second, anyway.

But I don't. I somehow manage to remain seated the whole journey – which, when you're flying as fast as Llew, doesn't take very long. We pass a group of giants marching in the direction of Rotwood, probably sent by Gawr to investigate what's going on once he realized the key was missing. We give them a wide berth, and soon Gawr's fortress comes into sight.

The giants who've remained behind are furious. They stomp and swipe at the trees as they try to find the stolen key. I feel a rush of fear for my friends, hiding in one of the nearby valleys. I hope they're safe. I hope none of the giants – or their feet – have found them.

But there, towering over all of them, is Gawr himself . . . and he looks *angry*. Oh boy, is he angry. He's kicking at the nearby hills like they're made of sand, leaving great foot-shaped gouges in them.

And there, hanging by a chain round his neck, is the Cariad.

It's a heart-shaped shield, just like Chief Cadwaladr's records showed, wrought in ancient metal, with a single red jewel at its centre. And while Gawr is massive, the shield still manages to cover a chunk of his torso.

I guess a shield enchanted to protect an entire land from magical chaos would have to be pretty big.

Gawr stills when he spots the sunlion, recognition

dawning on his face. We come to hover across the valley from him just as his lips curl at the corners. I can't call it a smile, because there's nothing remotely smiley about it: just wickedness twisted into the shape of one.

'Well, well, look who it is,' he booms. 'I thought I left you down in that dungeon to rot, little pussycat?'

A growl rumbles from Llew's belly. I can feel it vibrating beneath me. He's angry, too.

But then Gawr spots me and Cadno perched on Llew's back, and he starts making a deep, ugly noise, like caves crumbling and mountains splitting.

He's *laughing*, I realize.

'Ah, I see. Had a little help, did you?' Gawr spits. 'Pathetic. Look at that . . . three so-called legends together, and you'll still be no match for me.'

So-called legends . . . How does he recognize Cadno and me when he's been trapped in that dungeon for centuries?

'Oh yes, I know who you are, *Charlie the Legendary*,' Gawr snarls. 'I had my news sources, even locked up underneath Rotwood. In fact, my source might be somebody you know . . .'

He succumbs to another bout of that rock-grinding laughter. What is he on about?

'But enough of the pleasantries!' Gawr snaps. 'You're not going to be Charlie the Legendary for much longer. When I'm done with you, you'll be Charlie the Squashed!'

At that, Llew unleashes a furious roar. Part of me worries he might get so carried away with his rage that he'll forget Cadno and I are there and accidentally buck us off, sending us to messy ends on the ground, hundreds of metres below.

'Although, I must admit, I'm impressed that you managed to steal the key,' says Gawr, reaching up to scratch his head. 'How you managed that boggles my mind.'

'Doesn't take much,' I mutter, but Gawr hears me. He narrows his eyes and stomps a foot, making the peaks around us tremble.

'*What did you say?*' he shrieks.

'Nothing, nothing!' I call, and then, under my breath, 'Phwoar . . . Can't take a joke, can he?'

Gawr goes on. 'I even promised special freedoms to that little pipsqueak who stole the key for me,' he scoffs, and I frown. *Little pipsqueak?* Who is he on about? 'He was so tired of having to live in the shadow of the queen that he thought he'd have the last laugh. Came to me in the dead of night and told me all about how badly he's been treated up at that fancy palace, so I promised I'd help him if he helped *me*.'

That's when it hits home. All this time, we've been wondering how Gawr got out of his dungeon in the first place. And all this time, the answer has been sharing a roof with Branwen.

Prince Efnisien.

It makes sense now. A spoilt prince, jealous of the queen and her power, decides to form an alliance with the most terrible monster in the land. We've been wondering how somebody could possibly break into the palace to steal the key . . . but we never suspected somebody who already lives in the palace, especially not a *prince*. When we arrived at the palace to see Branwen, Prince Efnisien said he'd not long returned from his own travels – had he just got back from freeing Gawr?

And then another realization hits me, this one making me feel sick to my stomach.

He's never liked me since I beat him at archery when we were little, Branwen said. *He's not stopped practising since.*

Well, it looks like he got *very* good at archery. Good enough to even put a stop to the messenger who was racing to the palace to tell the queen about Llew's defeat. No wonder Prince Efnisien was trying to stop us from speaking to the injured man. He wasn't being caring – he didn't want us to find out any information!

Branwen is going to be absolutely *tamping* when she finds out.

'Little does he know that Gawr doesn't keep promises,' says the King of the Giants. He clicks his fingers, and a group of crafancs swoop from the entrance of his fortress, carrying between them an enormous wooden club. It's so huge that it takes at least twenty adult crafancs to carry it. They deliver it to their leader, who takes it from them and gives it a threatening swing through the air. It strikes a nearby hilltop, blasting it apart and sending a shower of rocks raining on to the forest below.

I gulp. He could do a lot of damage with that club.

'No, Gawr doesn't keep promises,' he repeats, 'apart from this one. I promise this will be the final time we face each other, ickle kitty, and that once I've finished you off, I'll have you stuffed like a teddy bear and mounted on the wall of my throne room.'

And then, before we can do anything to prepare, he's charging at us, with a bellow that could make the thunder cower. Llew dives at the last minute, and Gawr barrels past us with another swipe of his club. He turns, drool swinging from his mouth and an expression of hungry glee on his face.

'Or maybe I'll get you turned into a nice rug!'

He readies himself to charge again, and this time Llew gives me and Cadno a warning roar.

Hold on. I close my eyes and hold Cadno tight by pressing him into the back of the sunlion's neck, a hand grasping the mane on each side as Llew shoots upward.

The air around us judders violently as Gawr swings at us with his club, narrowly missing once again.

We enter into a deadly dance, in which Gawr charges and swipes, and we dip, dive, corkscrew, nip and dart to avoid each lethal blow. That's all Llew can manage – he hasn't yet fully recharged from being imprisoned, and it's still too cloudy for him to absorb more sunlight and rebuild his strength. And so he flits around in a constant race to dodge Gawr's never-ending attacks.

I close my eyes as the world rolls and turns, never staying still, the air slapping me in the cheeks between snatches of Gawr's dreadful face and his killer weapon.

He hasn't struck us yet, but it's only a matter of time. It's like we're a nuisance fly that he's swatting at. And what's worse is that while we might not be

getting clobbered, we're not exactly dishing out any damage, either.

We can't just keep doing this forever. Something's got to give eventually.

It turns out that something is me.

I've lost count of how many times we've dodged, but somewhere along the line I start to feel sick. It might be something to do with all the swirling and spinning and plunging, like I'm riding the world's longest, twistiest rollercoaster.

My cheeks bulge, and I know I'm going to throw up any second now if we don't stop.

I tap Llew's back as we level out after another dive, and it's like the sunlion reads my mind. He races to a nearby cliff that juts from a forest halfway up a peak and dumps me off – ungraciously, I might add, but I suppose he is busy battling a titan.

Cadno and I land with a dull thud as Llew returns to his enemy with a ferocious roar. The ground keeps moving underneath me, and I'm not sure if it's because I'm dizzy or if it's the shockwaves rippling out from

Gawr's thundering footsteps as he lunges in an attempt to swat Llew from the sky.

I lie there for a few seconds, waiting for the queasiness to ease, but then a familiar voice peals from the forest.

'Look! There he is! Charlie!'

Chapter 26

I lift my head, and what I see next fills me with hope —
the faces of my friends as they emerge from the forest's
edge. Roo, Lippy, Branwen, Blodyn and Pigog, alive
and well.

They hurry to my side, throwing themselves on
me with such force that I let out a warning groan.

'Careful,' I grumble. 'Feel sick. Too much looping.'

'Oh!'

They step away from me instantly, which is fair,
I suppose, their faces full of concern.

'You're all alive,' I croak. 'I was scared you'd been flattened.'

'We almost were,' says Branwen. 'But we managed to get out of the valley, and then we saw you return with Llew. We followed you from the ground.'

'What about the grizzlarth?' I ask, my voice hopeful.

Lippy shakes her head. 'He's awake, but definitely not ready to use his power again. He was too weak to follow us up this mountain to get to you.'

My heart sinks, my gaze sweeping over the skies to where Gawr and Llew are still locked in an endless clash. I wince as Gawr swipes his club, and this time it comes so close to striking Llew that the sunlion is sent careening through the air, on a blast of rippling wind. He recovers quickly, bolting back and jabbing at Gawr with his talons, tearing holes in the giant's clothes and shredding brilliant red slashes into his skin.

'Llew isn't getting a chance to use his hyperbeam,' I say. 'He needs sunlight so he can regain his full strength. We have to do something to help.'

'But what?' asks Roo despairingly. 'They're huge, legendary creatures and we're just . . . tiny humans.'

I grit my teeth. Because, in a way, he's right. We *are* just tiny humans. We don't have even a fraction of the size, strength or power these creatures have.

But what we *do* have is unmatched nerve.

You don't have to be anything special to be a hero. You don't need magical powers, or to be able to swing a sword (although Branwen would argue that it helps), or to be the size of a mountain. All you need is heart, a bit of fire, and some good friends.

And I've got those things by the bucketful.

'We might be tiny,' I say, sitting up, 'but that doesn't make us any less mighty.'

I quickly survey my surroundings. The battle is taking place in the bowl of another valley. Roo was right about one thing – we're too small to do any damage from here. What we really need is to get close to them. But how?

I study the peaks closest to us, and that's when I spot it: a waterfall, tumbling over the edge of a nearby precipice. It's high enough that it will put us on the same level as the battle. My gaze flickers to Blodyn, to her now-white fur and the spiderwebs of frost between her antlers.

'I know that face,' says Lippy. 'What are you thinking, Charlie?'

'It's a bit bonkers,' I say.

'The best ideas always are,' says Branwen. 'Like the hot-air balloon, remember?'

'Yeah, and look how that ended up,' says Roo, rolling his eyes at Pigog, who's draped round his shoulders.

'This one is *so* bonkers that it might just work,' I say. 'All we need to do is create a diversion, to give Llew time to go up above the clouds and recharge in the sun. Then he'll be able to use his power and finish Gawr off. OK, gather round and listen up, because this involves us all. A hero never acts alone.'

'This is completely bonkers!' Roo cries as we race up the mountain towards the waterfall.

'Yep!' I call back, Cadno running next to me. He's got sparks fizzing all over his body. I can feel the static through my trousers. 'Keep running!'

We get to the point where the river tumbles over the edge of the cliff, crashing into the valley below. From up here, we can see everything. The mountains and ravines stretching on for miles, now filled with giants watching their leader's battle against Llew with a sense of dreadful expectation, waiting for Gawr to deliver the final blow.

The battle rages on in the skies in front of us, but Llew looks like he's running out of energy, each swipe from Gawr's club getting closer and closer to hitting the mark. We have to do something, and fast.

My friends look at me, waiting.

'Just like we planned,' I say. 'Lippy?'

'OK, Blodyn, you're up!' says Lippy.

The frostdoe struts forward, placing her hoofs in the shallows of the river. She closes her eyes, and the water starts to freeze, hardening outwards from her feet until the whole river has turned to ice. The waterfall transforms into a solid pillar of white.

'Good job, Blodyn!' says Lippy.

'Well done, you two,' I say.

We carefully walk out on to the frozen surface of the river. Blodyn marches to the edge and this time extends the ice outwards, a bridge forming from the tip of the waterfall and stretching across the valley, creeping closer to Gawr and Llew's battle.

Once satisfied that the bridge is close enough, Lippy calls Blodyn off.

'Brilliant!' I shout. 'Now, Branwen!'

Branwen marches down the bridge and comes to a standstill near the end. She clears her throat, opens her mouth, and calls:

'Oi, Gawr! Over here, you ginormous donkey!'

Gawr pauses mid-swing and slowly turns, his eyes widening when he realizes who's standing in front of him. With Gawr's back turned, I give Llew a wink and watch as he shoots up, disappearing above the clouds, where the sunlight awaits him.

'*You!*' Gawr roars, spittle flying everywhere, some of the blobs so big that they form gooey ponds on the valley floor. I feel a flush of accomplishment. I knew the only thing that would get Gawr's attention away from Llew was his other sworn enemy – the queen of the land he wants so badly to claim for himself.

'Yes, it's me, Queen Branwen of Fargone.' She grins, hands poised on her hips. 'I hear you're trying to take over my queendom. What's that all about, eh?'

'It won't be your *queendom* for much longer,' Gawr spits. 'Once I'm finished with that blasted sunlion, you won't have anyone left to defend your precious land. Everything will be mine, and I'll –'

'Yeah, yeah, crush my bones to dust, blah, blah, blah,' says Branwen, suppressing an exaggerated yawn. 'We've heard it all before. Anyway, how *is* the battle going, hmm?'

Gawr blinks, like he's just remembered he was in the middle of something important, and turns – but the sunlion is gone. He flails around, a look of such confusion on his face that I almost laugh.

'Where is it?' he bellows, turning in a circle. 'Where did that stupid cat go?'

I smile as something drops through the clouds behind Gawr, a ball of light so bright it almost hurts to look at it. But then the ball unfurls wings, each and every feather gleaming like a gold ingot, and dives, coming to land before me and Cadno with a grace that Blodyn would be jealous of.

For the first time, I see Llew the sunlion as he is supposed to be. Tall, with a flowing golden mane and eyes that burn with the fire of a hundred fierce suns. His forelegs ripple with muscles, leading down to gigantic padded paws, his wings so big that he could wrap them round a bus and the tips would still touch. And then there are his back talons, which glisten like molten onyx, so sharp they could probably cut through marble.

'Feeling re-energized?' I ask the sunlion as Cadno and I climb aboard. I knew he'd be smart enough to take Gawr's distraction as an opportunity to disappear above the clouds, where the sunlight shines. And now here he is, looking stronger and mightier than ever.

'Not so many twists this time, all right?' I say, and then I give Llew an encouraging pat on the neck.

The sunlion takes off, and suddenly I'm airborne again. Gawr turns and, spotting us, peels his lips into the semblance of an ugly smile.

'Ah, there you are,' he growls, 'glowing like a pretty little fairy! Easier to see, easier to hit . . .'

He raises his club once again, but then Roo steps on to the ice bridge, Pigog sitting on his shoulder like a parrot.

'Oi, Gawr!' he calls.

Gawr pauses and whirls round. '*What now?*'

For a second, Roo looks tiny. Which, I suppose, he is, compared to Gawr. But then he clears his throat and says the words that we practised not so long ago.

'I just wanted you to know,' Roo calls, 'that I think your song and, by extension, *you* are really, really stupid. *Above* doesn't even rhyme properly with *sort of*, and putting *conquer* with *conker* was lazy! That was the worst chant I've ever heard!'

Gawr's cheeks turn red. One of his eyes twitches. And I . . . well, I grin even more widely. Because at the beginning of Gawr and Llew's battle, when he heard me make that snide remark about his intelligence, Gawr gave away his weakness: the biggest giant in all the land can't cope with being made fun of.

And how can you not make fun of a lyric like *Ground below and sky above, everything is mine – sort of*?

'How dare you, wretched human!' Gawr shrieks. 'Do you know who you're talking to? I will crush you like the pathetic little cockroach you are –'

'Charge your power, Llew,' I command as Gawr keeps hurling insults at Roo. 'Get ready.'

A deep hum rises from within Llew's chest. He opens his mouth, an orb of light forming inside which grows and grows. Llew's body vibrates with the power of it, with all the fire and heat and strength of the sun.

'Oi, Gawr!' I cry. 'Over here!'

Gawr turns, his furious gaze alighting on us and the hyperbeam building in Llew's mouth – and, for the first time since the battle began, he looks afraid. His mouth opens in a scream as I raise a fist into the air.

'Now, Llew!'

Llew unleashes his power, a beam of molten white light firing from his mouth and shooting directly towards Gawr. I'm ready to cheer with victory when my plan goes awry.

Because the beam doesn't find its target. Or, rather, it does – but it hits the Cariad square in the centre of Gawr's torso, and rebounds directly towards us.

The beam is moving with such speed that I don't have time to react. Instead, Cadno jumps into action, springing on to Llew's head, lightning sparking all over his body as he charges himself up and, before I can stop him, lets his power rip.

'Cadno, no!' I scream, but it's too late.

A lightning bolt explodes from his fur, more powerful than anything I've seen him produce so far, and crosses the space between us and the advancing hyperbeam. They collide in the middle, a crash of magical powers that seems to split the sky in two, and I watch in awe as they battle for space. They push against each other, sometimes inching towards us and then slowly creeping back towards Gawr.

'Hold on, Cadno!' I cry. I can see him closing his eyes, gritting his teeth in focus.

Gawr's face lights up as the mix of lightning and beam edges closer to us. Cadno's not strong enough to hold it for much longer. After everything we've been through, everything we've done, we're going to lose. The beam is going to rebound on us, and it will all be over.

I close my eyes and hold on tight, waiting for the inevitable to happen . . .

But it doesn't. I open one eye, terrified of what's happening – but what I see makes my mouth drop open.

Cadno's lightning has now pushed the beam almost all the way back to Gawr. I don't know how he's doing it, but it's working. He's growling, a continuous rumble sounding from his lips.

Gawr's expression falls.

'No!' he booms as his giant comrades watch on.

'You can do it, Cadno!' I shriek.

And then, with one final push, Cadno's lightning wins. The hyperbeam blasts back into the Cariad, this time with the force of Cadno's lightning mixed in. The Cariad splits in two, the magic barrelling into Gawr's chest, and the giant disappears behind an explosion so bright that I have to look away.

I hear his agonized scream, louder than anything I've heard in my life, and for a second I think my head might implode. But then the light fades, and a peculiar silence settles as Gawr falls backwards, slowly, and tumbles to the ground. He lands with such force that the mountains tremble around us. I'll be surprised if they don't feel the shock of his fall all the way over in Talarwen.

I wait, the awful anticipation squeezing my heart tight, but Gawr doesn't move again.

Chapter 27

'Charlie!' come the voices of my friends below, but I don't look at them. Not yet.

Cadno is lying on top of Llew's head, limp and unmoving.

'Cadno!' I cry as his body slides down into my open arms.

His eyes are closed. I don't know if he's breathing. Panic rises within my chest, worse than anything I've ever felt, a crushing terror that digs its claws deep into my soul.

'Help!' I scream. 'Help me!'

Immediately, Llew rushes to the riverbank where my friends wait. The frozen waterfall has already started to thaw, chunks of ice breaking free as the water begins to shift again underneath. I jump from the sunlion's back with Cadno in my arms, the rest of the crew crowding round me instantly.

'Charlie –' somebody says, but I interrupt.

'H-he's not moving!' I stammer. I hold my friend in my arms, but his eyes remain closed, his fur ashen and dull, devoid of even a hint of electricity or fire. There's nothing.

The light is gone.

'No,' I whimper, tears streaming down my cheeks. 'Cadno, please wake up.'

My friends go quiet. Nobody knows what to say, because nothing could have prepared us for this. I hold Cadno's head in my hands, running my fingers across his cheeks, and I lean down to press my lips to his usually squishy, wet nose. Now, it's dry.

Llew steps forward and lays his head on Cadno's chest. His warmth seeps into me, but it does nothing to combat the cold that's settling over my heart.

'Please, Cadno,' I sob. 'Please don't go.'

When Cadno doesn't respond, I close my eyes. A sorrow unlike anything I've ever felt before weighs on me. I don't know if I'll ever be able to shake off the darkness that I feel taking over my mind.

'Charlie,' Lippy hisses. 'Charlie, *look*!'

I open my eyes, and what I see is astonishing. Llew is crying, too, but instead of tears, golden light flows from the corners of his eyes. It runs down into Cadno's fur, enveloping his body in a glowing halo of sunlight. After a few seconds, Llew brings his head back up, and the light fades.

We wait, my heart beating so hard that I'm sure everybody must be able to feel it.

And then, Cadno blinks his eyes open. Two orange spheres stare up at me.

'Cadno!' I cry. 'You're awake! You're *alive*!'

Cadno blinks sleepily, then gives my nose a single lick with his dry, scratchy tongue – but it's easily the best cubby kiss I've ever received. Suddenly I'm embracing him, holding him so close that I'm surprised we don't become one, burying his snout into my neck as I wrap my arms round him. I never want to let go. I want to keep *cwtching* him forever.

'I thought I'd lost you.' I sniffle into his fur, and the little cub squeaks – probably because I'm holding him so tightly. 'Oh, sorry.'

I ease my grip, settling him back into a baby-like bundle in my arms, and look up at Llew.

'Thank you,' I say. 'I don't know how I can ever repay you.'

Llew bows his head and takes a step back. *You don't need to*, he's saying – and I can't help it. The happiness is so overwhelming that I laugh.

'I can't believe you did that!' I grin down at my four-legged companion. 'You almost killed yourself in the process, but you did that. *You* beat Gawr.'

I look up at my friends, who are staring down at me with happy smiles on their faces, their eyes still wet with tears.

'*We* did that,' I correct myself. 'We beat Gawr!'

'We're so glad Cadno is OK, Charlie,' Lippy sputters, a tear rolling down her cheek.

'Me too.' I glance back down at him. His eyes are closing again, already needing a nap. 'I think that's enough adventures for now.'

'Hey, what happened to his electric power?' asks Roo.

Wait . . . Roo is right. There doesn't seem to be any hint of electricity anywhere. No sparks, no flickering lightning. In fact, his fur looks . . . *normal*, like ordinary fox fur.

'I don't know,' I say. 'Hey, what about Blodyn?'

I seek out the magical deer, standing just beyond Lippy. It's with a sinking feeling that I realize that she's still white, her power still messed up even though Gawr is no longer using the Cariad to cause magical chaos.

But then . . . where is Cadno's power?

'His magic is gone,' I say quietly.

'Cadno's lightning broke the Cariad,' says Branwen. 'He gave his power so that he and Llew could win the battle. Maybe everything is stuck as it is now the Cariad's broken.'

I feel a swell of emotion. I remember all the chaos that Cadno and his flames has brought to my life. Singed socks and pillows, fire alarms going off, a whole clothes line up in flames. It hasn't always been easy looking after a firefox . . . but every second has been worth it. From the warmth as he *cwtches* into me at night, to the light he brings in the moments of darkness.

Cadno might not have his magic any more, but he's still magical to me.

I hold him tight. 'I don't care that your fire is gone. I'm just glad you're OK.'

Hey, at least Pa will be happy. He was always moaning about finding singed stuffed animals around the house.

'Guys, *look*!' Lippy whispers. 'Something is happening to Gawr!'

Our gazes sweep out to where Gawr lies at the head of the valley. The strangest thing is happening to him. His entire body – clothes, hair, skin, the lot – are losing the hues of life, and are slowly turning grey. But not just grey . . . *rocky*, as though the very hills are consuming him. And then grass begins to fur his legs, his feet, his arms, and trees sprout along his chest and his head, until after only a few short minutes there's no trace of Gawr at all, just a formation of hills and mountains which, if you squint just enough, looks a little like an enormous man having a sleep.

The only part of him that *hasn't* turned to stone is the Cariad itself, which now lies on the slope that was previously Gawr's chest, perfectly cleaved in two.

Roo gawks. 'W-what happened to him?'

'He turned into a mountain, you silly billy,' says Branwen with a roll of her eyes. 'That's what giants do. What, did you think mountains are just, like, *rock formations* or something?'

'Erm, yes?' we all say together, and I can't help but laugh at the wonder of Fargone and Wales, their histories so interlinked, our stories shared, rich with dragons and giants that turn into mountains. It's true what they say – that there's always a little bit of truth in legends.

Branwen snorts. 'You guys are so weird . . .'

She trails off as the ground starts to tremble. My heart stops, terrified for a second that Gawr is somehow shuddering back to life – but then I notice the other giants who watched our battle so closely from the surrounding mountains. They're all marching away, heads hanging low, getting smaller and smaller until they vanish from sight completely. With them go the crafancs, swarming across the skies as they flee.

'What was that all about?' asks Lippy.

'Their leader has fallen,' says Branwen. 'They're going back to the land beyond the mountains where they came from. Hopefully, they'll stay there forever. The giant invasion is over.'

'What about the crafancs?' Roo asks. Pigog timidly

follows the journey of the grown-up crafancs from his arms. 'Don't they live here?'

'I suspect they know they're no longer welcome in Fargone,' says Branwen, 'not after helping Gawr like that. And good riddance! I won't have any traitors in my queendom!'

Chapter 28

With Gawr defeated, we agree that our first stop should be a visit to our friends at the Warren.

'I'm sure the snabbits can do something about the broken Cariad,' says Branwen. 'They created it, after all. If they fix it, then maybe magic will go back to normal.'

Llew flies us all back to the Warren, even stopping to pick up the grizzlarth, who is still snoring under a tree, completely oblivious to the epic battle that has just taken place.

The snabbits are all gathered outside as we approach. They're bouncing and cheering, with the chief, chieftess and Teg at the forefront. They hurry forward to greet us as we land, showering us in confetti. The seahorses are there, too, still tooting lava bubbles into the air.

'Welcome back!' Chief Cadwaladr beams. 'I hear that a new mountain has formed to the east . . .'

'How do you know already?' I ask, Cadno still snoozing in my arms.

'Oh, I think all of Fargone felt the tremors of Gawr's downfall,' says Chief Cadwaladr. 'Well done, Charlie the Legendary. And well done, Llew. It's good to see you again.'

The chief salutes the sunlion, who bows his head in appreciation.

Teg steps forward and, tearing his admiring gaze from Llew for a moment, takes turns in giving us each a hug.

'Charlie, you did it!' he says, grinning.

'It wasn't just me,' I say. 'It was a group effort. A

hero never acts alone!'

Teg laughs. 'And you rescued the sunlion! Look at those golden locks. I wonder what shampoo he uses.'

His eyes alight upon Cadno, who's blinked one eye open to see what all the fuss is about. Teg's expression falls, concern taking over.

'Cadno,' he whispers fearfully, 'what happened to you?'

I explain what took place at the battle, how Cadno stepped in to save the day but lost his magic – and almost his life – when the Cariad shattered. Teg's eyes brim with tears.

'It doesn't matter,' he says, reaching out to ruffle Cadno between the ears. 'You'll always be a firefox to us. You helped defeat the Grendilock, Draig and then Gawr, after all.'

I smile, a pinch of sadness still gripping my heart, and hold Cadno tight.

'But what about the Cariad?' I say. 'It's broken, and everything is still so messed up . . .'

Chief Cadwaladr holds up a perfectly fluffed paw.

'Nothing us snabbits can't fix!' he declares. 'Although we will need to get to work right away. The sooner we can get the Cariad mended and in a secure new location up in the mountains, the sooner magic will return to normal . . .'

The snabbits hurry over to pick up the two halves that Llew had placed on the ground upon our arrival. They start heaving them away, ready to work their snabbit magic. Speaking of snabbits, there's one I haven't seen yet . . .

'Wait, where's Alba—'

'Coming through!' says a voice from deep in the crowd. There are a few gasps as somebody shoves their way forward. 'There's a new snabbit in town.'

The crowd parts, and a snabbit I've never seen before steps into the clearing. He's wearing jazzy black shades, and walking with a sort of rock-star swagger. He's got a glistening shell that's completely covered in what look like jewels. It's not until the snabbit reaches back and presses one of them that I realize they're *buttons*.

My mouth falls open as a pair of mechanical arms emerge from under the shell, one of them holding a hanky while the other removes the sunglasses from the snabbit's eyes. And that's when I realize – I *have* seen this snabbit before. In fact, I'm very familiar with him.

'*Albanact?*' Roo says, gawping. 'Is that you?'

'None other,' he says, as the robot hand with the hanky gets to work scrubbing his shades clean.

Roo fumbles for what to say. 'You look so . . . well . . . *different*.'

Albie smirks as the mechanical arm returns the

glasses to his face. 'Different? Look at me – I'm *dazzling.*'

'He's been insufferable ever since the snabbits finished his new shell,' Teg mutters to me. 'They added gadgets so he can be more practical, like a snabbit is supposed to be. He's got a dig function, a screwdriver function, an umbrella function . . . Honestly, the list goes on and on. The snabbits have truly outdone themselves, but they've created a monster.'

I gawp at a big gold button near the top. 'Ooh, what does this one do?'

Albanact lowers his shades and winks. 'Press it and you'll see.'

I press it and jump back in alarm when his shell starts to light up, beams in every colour jetting out like a disco ball. And there's music, too, blaring from somewhere inside, the sound of tribal drums and tambourines filling the air.

'That,' says Albanact proudly, 'is my Party Button.'

All around me, the snabbits start cheering and dancing.

'Now, let's celebrate the fall of Gawr!' Albanact announces, raising a fist into the air. The snabbit crowd screams in delight. 'Long live Albana— I mean, er, Fargone! Long live Fargone!'

It doesn't take long for the snabbits to fix the Cariad, which they carry into the clearing in a blaze of excitement. For something that's thousands of years old *and* recently split in two, it looks as good as new, glistening so pristinely that I can see my reflection in the metal.

'That was quick!' says Lippy. 'Albanact has only just stopped the disco!'

Albanact reclines against a nearby tree, pressing a button on his shell. A robotic arm emerges once again, this time holding a carrot for him to chomp. He looks very pleased with himself.

'It's not like we were building it from scratch,' Chief Cadwaladr says with a shrug. 'Just fusing it back together. Order should start returning to the land now . . .'

Miraculously, it does. Almost immediately, the seahorses stop producing lava bubbles, their former soapy ones filling the air instead. Kevin's hairdryer-snout switches back into a drill, which he gives a happy whizz. Blodyn's fur is already starting to return to its usual colour, the deep, wild emerald of the forest. The frost melts from her antlers, garlands of flowers slowly blooming instead, like they do upon the first warm whisper of spring.

'Blodyn!' Lippy beams. 'You're you again!'

She wraps her arms around the floradoe's neck. Blodyn closes her eyes and leans into the *cwtch*, making a daisy chain grow around her and Lippy.

'Pigog!' Roo cries as the baby crafanc takes a bold leap from his shoulder in a frantic bid to catch one of the seahorse bubbles. He hangs suspended in mid-air for a single heartbeat – then crashes to the ground. He lets out a shocked sound as Roo leans down to help him, then Roo jumps back with a yelp, his face dripping.

'He just splashed me!' Roo exclaims. 'He spouted water from his mouth!'

Sure enough, Pigog sprays another jet of water from between his tusks. It's a bit murky and green, like pond water, but it's water nonetheless.

'Looks like he's back to being an ordinary water-type crafanc,' says Branwen, her face lighting up.

It doesn't end there, either: the clock on the grizzlarth's belly switches back to a swirl. The big purple bear lets out a disappointed sigh when he realizes.

'You liked your time-stopping power, huh?' I ask. 'It's OK, buddy . . . you're still pretty cool to me.'

'Well, I, for one, am glad you can no longer freeze time,' says Branwen.

By my feet, Cadno whimpers as he watches his friends morph back into their magical selves. His eyes are heavy with sadness.

'Oh, Cadno,' I say, scooping him up and burying my face in his fur. 'You're amazing just the way you are.'

Cadno whines sadly, too heartbroken to take notice of my attempt at comfort.

'Now that the Cariad has been repaired, we should probably get going back to Talarwen,' says Branwen. 'I need to have a word with my cousin . . .'

She was, as I'd rightly predicted, *fuming* when I told her about Prince Efnisien. She used some very colourful language to describe how she was going to punish him. And I can't help remembering what she said about the crafancs: *I won't have any traitors in my queendom . . .*

'Llew,' she says, addressing the sunlion. 'Could you take us back to the city, please? And then you may return to the mountains with the Cariad. I've asked Chief Cadwaladr to build you both a nice new keep.'

Llew bows graciously, and I turn to face the snabbits.

'We can't thank you enough for everything you've done,' I say. 'I don't know how we'll ever repay you.'

'You saved the queendom,' says Chief Cadwaladr,

and then he adds, '*again*. Although maybe there *is* something . . .'

'What is it?'

'Well, maybe it is time that we snabbits start sharing more of our creations with the world,' says the chief, a paw poised thoughtfully on his chin. 'We've been hiding away in these hills for so long . . .'

'I'll make sure everybody knows what you've done for Fargone,' Branwen promises. 'We'll have a Great Exhibition in Talarwen to showcase your best inventions. And who better to organize it than my newest Royal Advisor . . . ?'

Albanact takes off his sunglasses – with his own paws, I might add – and blinks up at her. 'You . . . you weren't joking when you mentioned that before?'

'Absolutely not,' she says. 'As long as you stop being such a poser.'

Albanact stares for a moment, then tosses the shades aside and snaps to attention. 'This is an honour of the highest degree! Forgive me, Your Majesty, I don't know what came over me; I lost myself in the adoration of –'

'Yeah, yeah,' Branwen interrupts. 'We know. Now, come on, chop-chop. This queendom ain't gonna run itself.'

Chapter 29

As we soar over Fargone on our way back to Talarwen, it's clear that things really are returning to normal. I spot a starswan gliding gently past, its plumage once again black and purple, and swirling with studded stars. It loops around a crumbling Cantre'r Awyr cottage that's landed in the middle of a field. Slowly, the cottage starts to lift into the air on its island of earth, following the starswan as it returns to the skies. The human inhabitants, who seem to have been sleeping in a tent nearby, quickly jump up with jovial cries and hurry to climb on to the island before it gets too high.

And as Cantre'r Awyr rises back into the skies, so Gawr's fortress begins to sink, without the power of the Cariad to keep it in the air.

'What's going to happen to it?' Roo wonders aloud.

'It will fall eventually,' says Branwen. 'Might be best if we clear off before that happens. I'll issue a proclamation to make sure no one's underneath.'

The residents of Talarwen await us in the palace courtyard. They scream in a mix of shock and glee as they spot Llew coming over the walls. Some of them are holding up banners with things like *WE LOVE CHARLIE THE LEGENDARY* or *COME TO MY BIRTHDAY PARTY, ADVENTURE SQUAD* on them. They finally quieten down, waiting for their queen to speak.

'Fargone no longer has to worry about Gawr!' Branwen declares. 'The giants have been defeated, and Llew the mighty sunlion has been found. He will take the Cariad back to the mountains, where it will ensure that magical balance is maintained throughout Fargone until the end of time!'

The crowd starts cheering all over again, and Llew holds his head up high, his mane positively shimmering in the sun. They lap it up, basking in the sunlion's glory, but soon go quiet when Branwen speaks again.

'Now, where's Prince Efnisien?' she booms.

The heads of the crowd turn to a doorway set into one of the courtyard's stone walls. Standing there, looking down at the ground, is Prince Efnisien.

'Come here, cousin,' Branwen demands, and I gulp. What is she going to do to him? After all, he's almost single-handedly responsible for the near downfall of the queendom. If he hadn't stolen the key to the dungeon and freed Gawr, then none of this would have happened . . .

Prince Efnisien must be able to sense her fury, too, because he slowly peels himself away from the door and approaches, his head hanging. He comes to a stop in front of her.

'Look at me,' says Branwen, in her queen voice. Lippy squeezes my hand, and I squeeze back. I know we're both thinking the same thing . . . this is the first time we will ever see our friend use her power to punish somebody.

Prince Efnisien looks up and meets Branwen's gaze. He looks timid, mouse-like, all his former arrogance gone.

'You betrayed me,' says Branwen.

'No, Your Majesty, I d-didn't mean to –' the young prince stammers in panic, but Branwen raises a silencing hand.

'No more lies,' she says. 'I know what happened. Now is your chance to tell the truth. Prince Efnisien, why did you betray your queendom?'

The prince stares at her for a second. His lower lip wobbles, and his eyes take on a watery sheen that makes me think he's about to . . .

'Oh, Your Majesty!' he cries, throwing himself to the ground, his entire body racked with sobs. 'Forgive me, I beg you! I was jealous of your power and I thought I could do a better job of running the country, but I was wrong! I was wrong, OK? I should never have bargained with Gawr! I will regret it to the end of my days!'

Branwen's expression remains stony as she looks down at him.

'Thank you for your honesty,' she finally says. 'Your confession of treason has been noted. Now, stand up.'

The prince nods and gets to his feet, wiping his still-streaming nose. 'Are you going to punish me, Your Highness?'

'Oh, certainly.'

The prince nods. 'I guess I deserve it.'

'Yes, you do.'

He gulps. 'So, what's it going to be? Banishment? Prison? Are you going to lock me in Gawr's old dungeon for the rest of time? Oh, just tell me!'

'Oh, your punishment is going to be far, *far* worse than that,' says Branwen, and I watch as all the colour drains out of his face. 'Prince Efnisien,

I sentence you . . . to a *cwtch*.'

The prince winces, like he's just been slapped in the face. I have to admit, even I'm not sure I trust my ears.

He shuffles uncomfortably from foot to foot. 'I-I'm sorry . . . a *what*?'

'A *cwtch*. A very special person once told me they fix basically everything.'

And with that, Branwen puts her arms on his shoulders and tugs him into a tight, ferocious embrace. The prince gasps like he can barely breathe, but ultimately hugs her back.

'This . . . feels different to a normal hug,' he croaks over her shoulder.

'Yes,' says Branwen. 'This is how they do them in the magical land of Wales. I'm going to *cwtch* you until all the badness is gone.'

My friends and I beam at each other. Next to us, Cadno and Pigog perch on Blodyn's back, happily watching the scene unfold.

A few seconds later, Branwen releases the

prince. He stumbles back and rubs his neck like it's sore.

'There, that should do it,' she says, brushing her hands together. 'I forgive you, Prince Efnisien, but do *not* betray me again.'

The prince nods solemnly. 'Yes, Your Majesty. I mean, no, Your Majesty.'

'I am a generous queen,' says Branwen. 'You are dismissed.'

Prince Efnisien dips into a bow, as Branwen speaks again.

'Oh, and Effy?'

Efnisien freezes. 'Yes, Your Majesty?'

'I'm also appointing you Royal Toilet Cleaner for the foreseeable future.'

The prince bolts upright, an expression of horror

on his face. '*What?* N-no, you can't! Anything but that –'

Queen Branwen quirks an eyebrow, and her cousin peters out into silence.

'Very well, Your Majesty.'

He bows again and disappears back into the palace. Meanwhile, we flock around Branwen.

'That was very kind of you, Branwen,' says Roo. 'I'd have had him hanging from his toes in a dungeon after what he did!'

Branwen smiles softly. 'A good monarch is remembered for their acts of kindness, not cruelty.'

'I thought you did a *wonderful* job,' says Lippy. She leans in to kiss Branwen on the cheek at the same time that Branwen turns her head, and their lips accidentally meet, just for a second. Their eyes widen and they leap away from each other, blushing furiously.

'Sorry,' they both mumble, and then giggle nervously.

'Actually, if you have a minute, Lippy, I'd like to

ask you a question,' says Branwen. Lippy nods, a confused look on her face.

Teg clears his throat. 'Right, well, Charlie and Roo, fancy coming to check up on the Gallivant Menagerie with me? It might have descended into farce by now.'

Roo and I exchange meaningful glances as Teg chivvies us in the direction of the carriages. I have a pretty good idea what Branwen might want to ask Lippy. The question is: what's her answer . . . ?

Chapter 30

The Gallivant Menagerie has been moved to a quiet corner of the palace grounds while we've been away, where some of Branwen's attendants have been doing their best to care for the animals. Teg sags with relief when he sees that the train of carriages is still intact, and that their inhabitants aren't running amok like they were a few days ago.

The creatures crowd happily around Teg as he goes about checking them all one by one.

'Everybody seems to be doing well,' he says, but

then pauses. 'Although, wait. There's still some left to check.'

He takes us to the hospital carriage, where the wotters have descended from their perch near the ceiling and are now resting at the bottom of a great tank of water in the corner.

'Ah, they're back to being water types,' says Teg, with a smile. 'Balance has been restored.'

'They still don't look very happy,' I say. It's true: the pair are still curled up in a tight embrace, as though they're trying to comfort one another.

'You're right. Unfortunately, I don't know how to fix that. All they want is some young of their own, but seeing as they're both female, they can't . . .' Teg pauses, a look of realization dawning on his face. 'Wait a minute . . .'

'Teg, what is it?' I ask.

'I have an idea,' he says. 'It might be a bit bonkers, but –'

'The best ideas usually are,' I finish for him. 'Come on, out with it!'

Teg whirls round to face Roo, who's got Pigog sitting directly on top of his head.

'Do you think your parents would welcome Pigog into your home, Roo?' he asks, and Roo's eyes widen.

'I hadn't thought about that,' he says. 'But no way. They'll freak! They don't even know about Cadno or any of this magic stuff!'

'So would you say that taking Pigog back to Wales with you is a bit . . . challenging?' Teg presses.

Roo looks torn. 'I . . . I guess so. I don't see how I can.'

His eyes get watery, and he scoops Pigog into his hands, before bringing him down to cradle him. My heart goes out to them. Roo and Pigog have been on quite the journey in their brief time together.

'What am I going to do?' he wails. 'I don't want to leave him behind. I *love* him. And he needs *someone* to look after him.'

Teg crosses his arms, eyebrows quirked as he waits

for realization to settle in. When it does, Roo lets out a gasp.

'Wait . . . are you suggesting I leave Pigog with the *wotters*?'

Teg shrugs. 'You've looked after Pigog so well, Roo, but you can't take him home with you. The wotters desperately want a child of their own. It could be the perfect solution. You'll know he's always going to be safe and loved, and you can visit whenever you want.'

'I don't know,' says Roo, his voice quivering. He looks down at Pigog, who's staring adoringly up at him.

'Think about it, Roo,' I say. 'It's like you've been Pigog's foster carer while he was in need, and now the wotters are going to adopt him.'

Roo still looks unsure. 'Like . . . like you?'

'Yes,' I reply, with a smile. 'Like me.'

Roo ponders a second, but finally nods. 'All right,' he agrees. 'I think it could be a good idea. What do you think, Pigog?'

Pigog reaches up and licks his companion's cheek, then turns his attention to the wotters, who have woken from their doze and are staring at us through the glass of the tank with big, curious eyes.

'Shall we introduce them?' asks Teg, a glimmer of excitement in his eyes.

Roo takes a deep breath. 'OK.'

He carries Pigog over to the tank and gently props him on the edge. We watch as the wotters glide up to the surface, lifting their heads above the water to study him more closely. Pigog lets out an excited snuffle and wriggles his butt, like he wants to splash into the water right away.

But Roo clings to him, giving the wotters space to contemplate. They turn to each other, eyes wide, almost like they're talking to each other using their minds. I wonder what they're saying. I cross my fingers, desperately hoping that they're deciding together that they want to adopt Pigog . . .

And then they reach up with their paws and open

their mouths, calling to the baby crafanc in a sweet, gentle song.

'They approve!' Teg exclaims. 'Roo, let him into the tank.'

Roo leans down, but before Pigog departs, the baby crafanc looks back up at him, reluctance creeping into his eyes.

'It's OK,' Roo encourages him, tears brimming in the corners of his own eyes. 'You can go. They'll look after you, I promise. They're going to be your mummies. I'll come back and visit you all the time; don't you worry about me.'

Pigog blinks, then turns and plops gracelessly into the water. The wotters twirl around him, all of them studying each other for a few seconds . . . and then the most wonderful thing happens.

They embrace.

The wotters place their heads next to Pigog's and press around him, and all three creatures close their eyes in happiness.

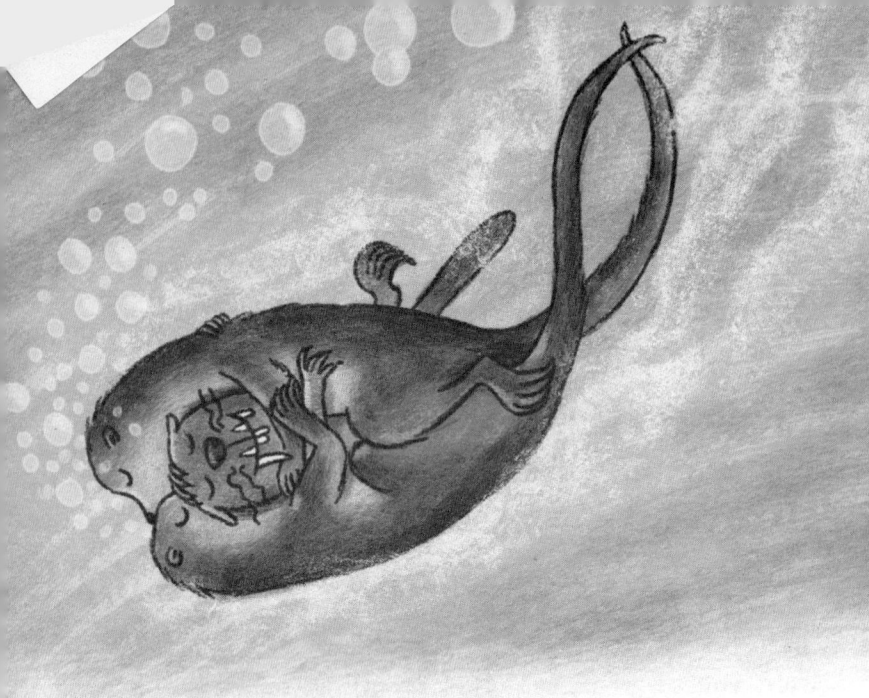

'They'll make wonderful mothers,' Teg says, beaming proudly.

'They already are,' says Roo, who looks both happy and sad at the same time. 'Brilliant idea, Teg –'

Lippy appears in the doorway, Blodyn just behind. Her expression is worried, breaking the dreamy enchantment that has settled over us.

'There you are,' she says, panting. 'I've been looking all over for you. One of the servants said a bird just brought this letter to the palace. It's from your dads, Charlie.'

I rush over, snatch the letter and drink up the words that are scrawled upon it.

Charlie,

The three of you need to come home RIGHT NOW. The dam is about to burst and they're evacuating everybody in Bryncastell. Get your butts back quick!

Dads x

I look up. Lippy and Roo are both waiting, their shoulders tense.

'The dam's about to burst,' I say, my voice deathly quiet. 'We need to go home.'

Lippy's eyes widen. 'Oh no.'

'Yes,' I reply. 'Hurry. We've got to get back to the portal.'

Lippy and I hurry to the doorway, but Roo remains behind, frozen to the spot.

'Roo!' I hiss. 'What are you doing? Didn't you hear me? We need to go!'

'I'm just thinking . . .'

'Now's not the time to think!'

'But I have an idea,' he says, his brow furrowed. 'It's a bit bonkers, but . . .'

My heart flutters with hope. 'Yes, yes, all the best ones are, I know! All right, spit it out.'

Roo smiles. 'Crafancs are good at building things, right?'

'Yes,' says Teg uncertainly.

'Specifically, they're good at building dams in rivers, right?'

'Yes, but I don't understand –' Teg starts, and then Lippy interrupts, her mouth wide in admiration.

'Oh my goodness, Roo!' she exclaims. 'That's it! You're a genius!'

'Come on,' I say. 'Roo, grab Pigog. Teg, grab the wotters. We're going back to Wales.'

Chapter 31

One frantic deer-ride later, Teg, Lippy, Roo and I step back through the portal and into Wales. The sky is still a bruised ceiling of moody-looking clouds, but the rain has stopped.

'Looks like we were right about the Cariad being responsible for the rain here,' I say. 'The magical chaos from Fargone leaked into our land and messed all the weather up. Now that Gawr has fallen, the rain in Wales has stopped.'

'Still too late for the dam, though,' says Lippy,

worry crossing her features. 'We need to get down there, and fast.'

We get back on the deer and set off, our home town coming into sight beneath us. From up here at the castle, it's easy to see that the situation has worsened since we left a few days ago. The river has burst its banks completely and the fields surrounding Bryn-castell have turned to a sea of brown water. The streets have all become rapids, flashing lights blaring as fire engines attempt to evacuate people from their homes. I know that Dad will be out there helping, and I can only hope he's safe.

'This is bad,' I say. 'This is really bad.'

It doesn't take long to get to the dam. We come to a stop on the swollen banks of the reservoir, watching water rushing over the top and crashing into the valley below. Halfway down the dam, we can see the jet of water spouting from a hole in the wall. The whole thing keeps making an ominous groaning sound.

'All right,' I say. 'We've got to act, and we've got to act fast. Roo?'

Roo nods, his mouth set in a determined line. 'All right. Pigog, I need you and your new mums to work your magic. Block the hole so that the dam won't break.'

Pigog yelps in understanding and then seems to consult with his mothers, who are both coiled round Teg's shoulders, through a series of squeaks and grunts. They leap into action, diving into the water together and out of sight.

We wait in tense silence, with no idea what's going on below the surface. I brace myself for the dam to crumble at any second, for the entire contents of the reservoir to go crashing down the valley and wash away Bryncastell like a little model village.

An age seems to pass, in which none of us so much as glances away from the surface for a second. But then, suddenly, the roar of the water gets quieter.

We look at each other, our expressions hopeful. Does that mean . . . ?

'Let's go check!' I say, hopping off my deer. I race along the bank with my friends hot on my tail, and look down at the dam. There's still a lot of water thundering over the top, but the powerful jet that erupted from the hole in the middle of it has gone.

'They did it!' Roo exclaims, and then we're all hugging and jumping up and down just as Pigog and his wotter mums emerge from the water and come scrambling up the bank. They might not have air powers any more, but that doesn't stop them from diving into our open arms.

'Eurgh!' Lippy shrieks with glee. 'You're all wet!'

But we don't care. We're too busy celebrating. There's still a lot of water about, but at least Bryncastell won't be swept away, or become another drowned village for the Welsh legends. Blodyn and Cadno dance together in a circle, the other Fargone deer swinging their antlers like they're cheerleading.

When we finally break apart, Teg regards us with one of the widest grins I've ever seen.

'What are you staring at, Teg?' I tease.

'Just look at you lot,' he replies. 'When I first

brought Cadno to you, Charlie, you wouldn't even say boo to a goose.'

'Literally,' I say, thinking of the ferocious geese down at the lake who regularly used to petrify me.

'The three of you have gone from defeating the Grendilock, to saving Fargone, to saving Fargone *and* Wales from destruction,' he says. 'What will you do next, eh?'

'Rest!' I cry. 'I don't want another adventure for a very, *very* long time.'

'Adventure Squad on break!' says Lippy, grinning.

Teg throws his head back and laughs. 'Are you sure?'

'Sure!' Roo and Lippy retort.

'Me too,' I say. 'Come on, Teg. We'd best get you guys back to Fargone. We need to go home.'

We return to the portal on deerback once again, and already we can see that the flow of water over the dam has lessened. It will be a while before the water drains out of Bryncastell, but at least it's not going to get any deeper.

However, I *do* notice some new trees appearing as we ride. 'Blodyn,' I call to the floradoe, who looks suspiciously like she's concentrating. 'What are you doing?'

Blodyn looks away, denying any responsibility.

'Trees are one of the best flood defences,' says Teg from the back of his own deer. 'Very good for drinking up all this water! Clever, Blodyn.'

'Hey, do you guys want to know what Branwen wanted to speak to me about?' Lippy asks as we cross into the grounds of the castle. Her eyes glitter with excitement.

'Go on, then,' I say, but I have a feeling I already know.

'She asked if I wanted to be her *girlfriend*!' Lippy squeals. 'And I said *yes*!'

Roo and I grin. Blodyn lets out a celebratory bleat.

'Awh, congratulations, you two,' says Roo. 'Wild that you're going out with a queen. She's going to give *such* good birthday presents.'

'I know! Wait, does this make me a princess or

something?' Lippy stops short, looking a bit green. 'Eurgh! I've never wanted that!'

'Maybe you can be a warrior princess,' I offer. Lippy seems happy with my suggestion, and we walk Teg, Pigog, the deer and the wotters to the portal on a floaty cloud of contentment.

'Take good care of Pigog and his new family,' says Roo as Teg comes to a standstill before the curtain of ivy.

'Don't you worry, I will,' Teg replies. 'I'm going to find the most beautiful, most peaceful lake for them to nest in and get to know each other as a family.'

I beam as Pigog's wotter mums nuzzle him, shooting happy bubbles from their mouths which Pigog then scurries after, trying to burst them with the plates on his back. Blodyn marches next to them, a garland of sunflowers blossoming round her neck.

'Tell Branwen we'll be over to visit soon,' I say, and the floradoe bows her head.

We say our goodbyes, and Roo sniffs as he hands Pigog back to Teg after giving him a final cuddle.

'Hey, it's OK,' I assure him. 'You'll see Pigog again soon.'

Roo wipes his nose. 'I know . . . I just . . . I'll just miss him, is all.'

Lippy puts her arm round his shoulders. 'Of course you will. You formed a bond. We all have. But that bond is unbreakable, and it will be even stronger when you see him again.'

Roo nods, and Teg, Blodyn, Pigog, the wotters and the deer step up to the portal together.

'Farewell, heroes of Fargone,' says Teg with a wave. 'I'm sure we'll meet again . . . hopefully just for a nice cup of tea.'

'Yeah, none of this whole saving-the-world business,' I say.

Teg grins, and disappears through the ivy with the wotters on his shoulder and Pigog in his arms, followed by the deer. Blodyn gives us a final bow goodbye, and then she's gone, too.

I sigh. 'Well, now that's over, let's head home. I bet my pa is losing his mind.'

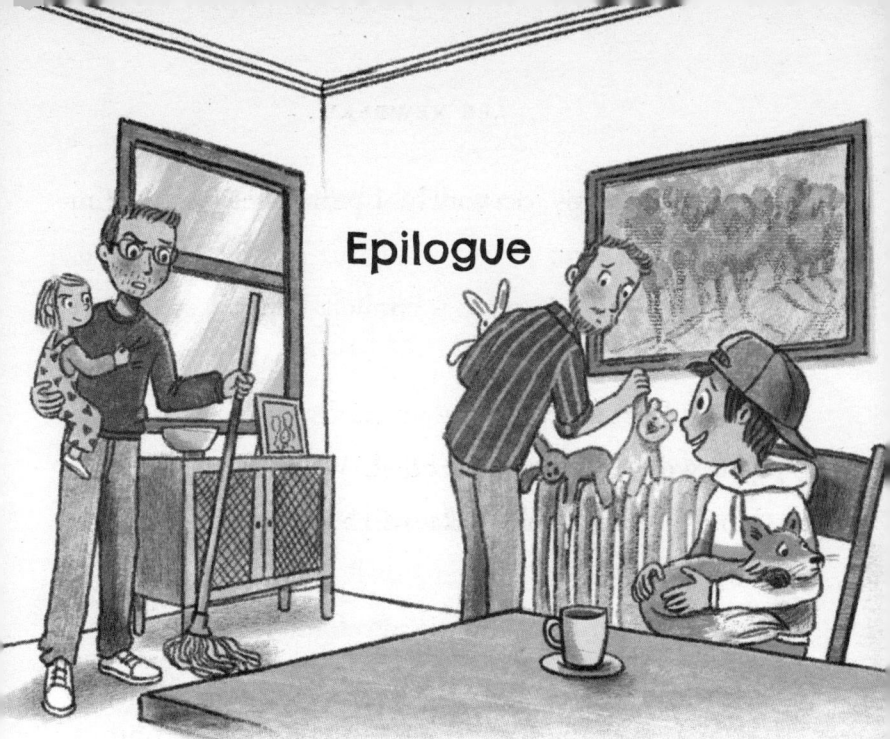

Epilogue

'I find it rather *odd* that the dam somehow managed to fix itself just a few minutes before you guys arrived home from Fargone.'

Pa is eyeing me suspiciously as he mops the kitchen floor a few days later, holding Edie on his hip. The floodwaters are already dropping all over Bryncastell and the evacuation has been suspended. Luckily, our house escaped any major damage, although Dad reckons we'll need new carpets.

'I know, it is a bit strange, isn't it?' I say, smiling

widely. Perhaps too widely. I probably look like I'm keeping a secret . . . which I sort of am, I suppose. 'But let's not question it too much. Don't want to jinx it, do we?'

'And you say that Cadno just *lost* his powers while you were having your fun sleepover at the palace?' asks Dad, who didn't take the news that our firefox is now an ordinary fox very well. He actually cried – which is weird, because, as a firefighter, he's supposed to put out fires, not *cwtch* them.

I guess that's just the spell Cadno's fire had on us all. Even Pa grew to love it. I often used to find Cadno snuggled up on his lap at the end of the night, while he and Dad were watching some crime documentary together on TV.

'Yep,' I say meekly. 'Teg said that sometimes happens to firefoxes. They just, er . . . lose their flames and become ordinary foxes.'

'And what about the electricity? Did Teg have an explanation for that?'

'He . . . er . . . he said that it was a defence

mechanism against all the rain,' I say quickly. 'Sometimes firefoxes will shed their flames if they're around too much water and turn into something else.'

Dad looks impressed. 'It's like he evolved,' he says.

Cadno growls in protest. My dads both raise their eyebrows.

'Anyway, can we not talk about it in front of Cadno? He's still a bit upset about it all.'

That part, at least, is true. Cadno hasn't been the same since we got home. He just slinks around with his tail between his legs and a miserable look on his face. I'd never considered that animals could have broken hearts before, but now I know they can.

'Oh, of course,' says Dad. 'Sorry, Cadno, didn't mean to be insensitive. You'll always be our special firefox, flames or no flames.'

'That's what I told him.'

I know it's bad to lie to your parents, but I don't think they'd ever let me go to Fargone again if they knew the truth – that we fell from the sky in a hot-air balloon, almost got squished by tumbling castles, faced off against a twisterantula, found a lost sunlion, and finished with a deadly battle against the biggest, most violent foe I've ever had the displeasure of meeting.

Yeah, somehow I don't think that would go down well.

I think they know something is up, but if they do, they choose not to ask about it. They're just happy I'm back, that the rain has gone, and that the threat looming over Bryncastell has faded.

So Pa keeps mopping, Dad keeps draping Edie's stuffed animals over the radiators to dry, and, over the next few days, we settle into our new reality as an ordinary family who just so happens to have a pet firefox . . . minus the fire part.

'So they just . . . believed you?' asks Roo.

We're up in my tree house, somewhere we've not been since before the rain started. Everything is still a bit soggy, but it feels good to be back. We spent hours up here when Cadno first came to Wales, playing games and planning how to keep him safe and secret.

Things are different now, but also the same. Sure, Cadno doesn't have his flames any more, but he's still an adorable little idiot. Right now, for example, he's stalking a snail that's creeping across the floor, front paws flat on the ground, butt pointing into the air, tail swishing and nose wiggling inquisitively.

'I don't think they were a hundred per cent convinced,' I say, 'but they decided not to question it. What about your parents?'

'Mine still think I was at yours,' says Roo.

Lippy, who's been quiet for a while, suddenly blurts out, 'I told my mum about Fargone!'

'You *what*?'

'I know!' she cries. 'I just . . . I couldn't hide the fact that I have a girlfriend from her, could I? I tell my mum everything! So then she obviously asked who she is and where she's from . . . and then it all just came pouring out!'

'*Ooo-kay*,' I say, trying to sound calm. 'And what did she say?'

'Well, she already knows about Cadno, so she

didn't have a hard time believing it,' says Lippy. 'But she does want to sit down and *have a cup of tea* with your dads, Charlie. She knows they've been to Fargone and I think she wants to ask them about it.'

I sigh. 'Right, I'll let them know.'

'Speaking of Cadno,' says Roo. 'How're you finding life without the flames?'

'Much quieter,' I say, watching as Cadno leans in close to the snail. 'I think he's slowly making his peace with it.'

'Oh, Charlie,' says Lippy. 'I'm sure he'll get back to normal.'

'Yeah,' I say. 'I do miss his flames, but he's still the same old Cadno. Still as cuddly and curious and mischievous as ever . . .'

Cadno's nose touches the snail, and the little critter quickly withdraws into its shell. This is Cadno's first close encounter with a snail, so he snaps his head back in alarm, too – and a shimmer of light flickers over his body.

There one second and gone the next.

When I look up, both Lippy and Roo are wide-eyed.

Lippy nods. 'Surely not . . .'

'Make him do it again!' Roo whispers.

Cadno's already on high alert after the snail's party trick, so I prod him – he jolts to attention, and another wave of hot, bright light ripples over his body, so quickly that I could almost have imagined it.

'You guys . . . did you just see what I saw?'

'I think so,' Lippy says in astonishment.

I nod happily. It was hardly a wildfire – more of an ember – but I don't mind. It'll grow.

Fire is fire.

Acknowledgements

When I first set out to write *The Last Firefox*, I only had one story in mind – but I soon discovered that there were more adventures awaiting Charlie, Cadno and their friends. So one book turned into two, and then, finally, into three. A trilogy! I can hardly believe it. I wrote a trilogy! But, as with the first two books, *The Lost Sunlion* didn't just spring from my fingertips and then jet straight off to the printers. Oh no. There's a small army of people who helped me realize this story, and these are the people I'd like to thank.

My thanks, first, to my amazing agent, Amber Caraveo. I've come a long way since that first messy manuscript I sent you back in 2015, and you have helped to shape me into the author I am today. Thank you for being one of my biggest cheerleaders!

ACKNOWLEDGEMENTS

I still find myself staring in disbelief at that adorable little bird in the corner of my book covers — and so a multitude of thanks to everybody at Puffin, the publisher of my dreams. Thank you to my editor, Ben Horslen, who has not only helped to sculpt my stories into something readers would love, but for also making the whole experience extraordinarily fun and worry-free. And to Phoebe Williams, for doing such a tremendous job with getting my name out there and for making sure I always got from A to B without catastrophe, and for always pointing me to the nearest toilet! To Jan Bielecki and Mandy Norman, for helping to make *The Lost Sunlion* look amazing, and to Josh Benn for overseeing the editorial process with an expert eye.

I don't feel like an ordinary thank you is quite enough for the next one, so I'm going to shout it: THANK YOU to Laura Catalán. I count myself so lucky to have been paired with such a wonderful illustrator. Your artwork has truly made these stories soar. Thank you, thank you, thank you.

ACKNOWLEDGEMENTS

There are also a lot of people in my personal life who have championed me every step of the way. To my author friends, especially everybody in the Team Skylark WhatsApp group, thank you. And Lesley Parr, my fellow Welshie, I love you dearly.

To my wonderful friends, for always asking for updates and then, consequently, your patience when I no doubt went off on a huuuuuge unabridged version of my publishing journey. And an extra special shout-out to Cerian McDowall, for being there for me always. Not just through the book writing, but also the messy life stuff – the two often seem to feed into each other. You're my soul sister.

Thank you to my family, to Mammy, and Lindsey and Daniel. You've all been there for me since I first declared I wanted to be an author at eight years old, and I don't think I could have done it without your steadfast belief.

This next one means an awful lot. Thank you, eternally, to you, Tom. Things might have changed between us, but many things, simultaneously, have stayed the same: first, your confidence in and support of me, but also that part of us that remains family. And that, ultimately, is what these books are all about.

And finally, my biggest thanks goes to my son, Parker. These stories boil down to you. Everything boils down to you. Thank you for being my reason.

ENJOY ALL OF CHARLIE AND CADNO'S ADVENTURES

THE LAST FIREFOX SERIES IS ALSO AVAILABLE ON AUDIOBOOK

READ BY
CALLUM SCOTT HOWELLS